"I don't unc

plaintively.

"If you're attracted to me—"

"I'm more than just attracted," Rick interrupted. "I'm obsessed. Just being with you is no longer enough, and a short-term relationship would bring more anguish than pleasure when it ended."

"But why would it have to end? I mean if we…if we learned to love each other—"

Rick sighed. "You don't *learn* to love. Either it happens or it doesn't, and marriage for us is out of the question."

Her head jerked up then. "What is it that makes it so impossible?"

Rick imagined the scorn she would feel for him when he told her the truth.…

Dear Reader,

What a special lineup of love stories Silhouette Romance has for you this month. Bestselling author Sandra Steffen continues her BACHELOR GULCH miniseries with *Clayton's Made-Over Mrs.* And in *The Lawman's Legacy*, favorite author Phyllis Halldorson introduces a special promotion called MEN! Who says good men are hard to find?! Plus, we've got Julianna Morris's *Daddy Woke up Married*—our BUNDLES OF JOY selection—*Love, Marriage and Family 101* by Anne Peters, *The Scandalous Return of Jake Walker* by Myrna Mackenzie and *The Cowboy Who Broke the Mold* by Cathleen Galitz, who makes her Silhouette debut as one of our WOMEN TO WATCH.

I hope you enjoy all six of these wonderful novels. In fact, I'd love to get your thoughts on Silhouette Romance. If you'd like to share your comments about the Silhouette Romance line, please send a letter directly to my attention: Melissa Senate, Senior Editor, Silhouette Books, 300 E. 42nd St., 6th Floor, New York, NY 10017. I welcome all of your comments, and here are a few particulars I'd like to have your feedback on:

1) Why do you enjoy Silhouette Romance?
2) What types of stories would you like to see more of? Less of?
3) Do you have favorite authors?

Your thoughts about Romance are very important to me. After all, these books are for you! Again, I hope you enjoy our six novels this month—and that you'll write me with your thoughts.

Regards,

Melissa Senate
Senior Editor
Silhouette Books

Please address questions and book requests to:
Silhouette Reader Service
U.S.: 3010 Walden Ave., P.O. Box 1325, Buffalo, NY 14269
Canadian: P.O. Box 609, Fort Erie, Ont. L2A 5X3

THE LAWMAN'S LEGACY

Phyllis Halldorson

Silhouette

ROMANCE™

Published by Silhouette Books
America's Publisher of Contemporary Romance

For Jiggs. Happy special anniversary, sweetheart.
I'm so glad I married you and got it right the first time.

SILHOUETTE BOOKS

ISBN 0-373-19255-X

THE LAWMAN'S LEGACY

This edition published by arrangement with Harlequin Books S.A.

Printed in U.S.A.

Books by Phyllis Halldorson

Silhouette Romance

Temporary Bride #31
To Start Again #79
Mountain Melody #247
If Ever I Loved You #282
Design for Two Hearts #367
Forgotten Love #395
An Honest Lover #456
To Choose a Wife #515
Return to Raindance #566
Raindance Autumn #584
Ageless Passion, Timeless Love #653
Dream Again of Love #689
Only the Nanny Knows for Sure #760
Lady Diamond #791
More Than You Know #948
Father in the Middle #1060
Mail Order Wife #1133
A Wife for Dr. Sam #1219
The Lawman's Legacy #1255

Silhouette Special Edition

My Heart's Undoing #290
The Showgirl and the Professor #368
Cross My Heart #430
Ask Not of Me, Love #510
All We Know of Heaven #621
You Could Love Me #734
Luscious Lady #764
A Haven in His Arms #863
Truly Married #958
The Bride and the Baby #999

Silhouette Books

Silhouette Christmas Stories 1991
"A Memorable Noel"

PHYLLIS HALLDORSON

met her real-life Prince Charming at the age of sixteen. She married him a year later, and they settled down to raise a family. A compulsive reader, Phyllis dreamed of someday finding the time to write stories of her own. That time came when her two youngest children reached adolescence. When she was introduced to romance novels, she knew she had found her long-delayed vocation. After all, how could she write anything else after living all those years with her very own Silhouette hero?

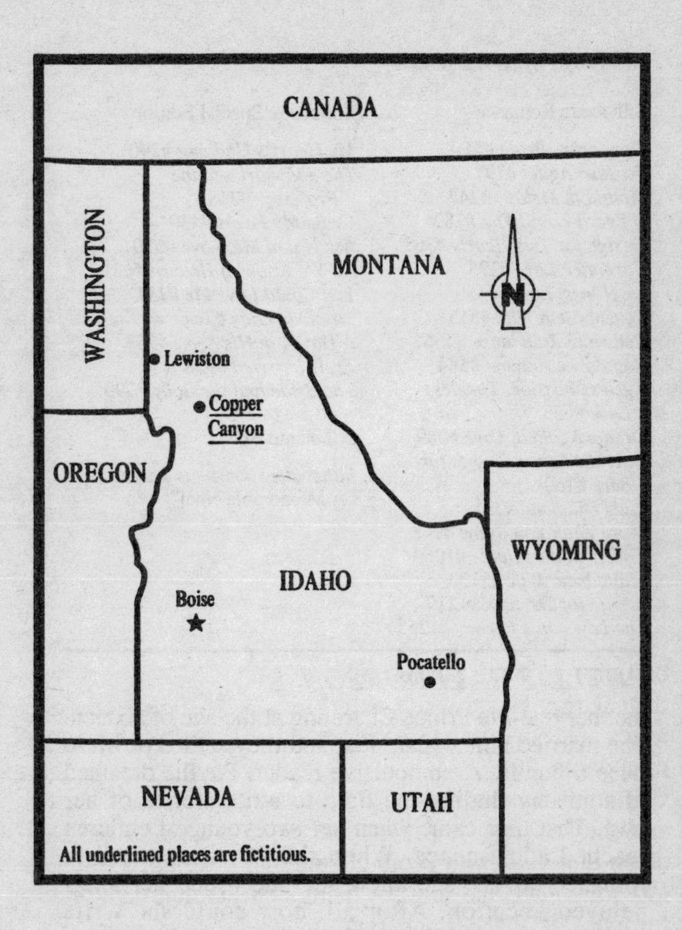
CANADA
WASHINGTON
MONTANA
N
Lewiston
Copper Canyon
OREGON
WYOMING
IDAHO
Boise
Pocatello
NEVADA
UTAH
All underlined places are fictitious.

Chapter One

Even through the pouring rain Jodi Hopkins could read the road sign. It said Red Robin Lane, but there must be a mistake!

She made a left hand turn and stopped at the curb. This couldn't be the street where her great-aunt Aretha Coldwell had lived. Red Robin Lane was such a pretty name. It brought to mind images of pastel-colored cottages with thatched roofs and white picket fences, and children riding trikes and bikes and throwing balls at hoops above the garage doors.

But this street was dreary. It was on the outskirts of town, and the houses, what few there were, were big, old, run-down buildings with peeling paint and unkempt yards. The lots were huge and most of them were littered with broken furniture, appliances and cars.

She shuddered. There were only two buildings on this side of the block—the one she was parked in front of, which was number 900, then a gaping hole carpeted with mud and uncut strawlike grass and then another building that was almost hidden by trees and brush at the other end. Surely that one wasn't Aunt Aretha's!

A gust of wind shook the car as she took her foot off the brake and guided it slowly down the block to stop again in front of the jungle of twisted vines and branches that nearly obliterated the view of the dilapidated house from the curb. Taking a deep breath she shut off the engine. If there was a number on the house it wasn't visible from the street. She'd have to look for it at closer range.

The cold tempest blasted her when she opened the door, and she pulled the hood of her waterproof parka over her head as she reluctantly stepped out into the downpour. Walking briskly she made her way up the broken cement walkway and through the overgrown brush to the front door.

The heavy black clouds had turned the afternoon dark and dreary, and the snapping Idaho squall whipped chilling sheets of water around her as she fought to keep her balance. This was a creepy place, and she was the world's biggest coward. Even as a child she'd been terrified of the masks and jack-o'-lanterns at Halloween, and now, as an adult, she couldn't read Stephen King or Dean Koontz novels because they made her break out in a cold sweat.

So what was she doing here! Why didn't she get in her car and hightail it back to her pretty little house in Cincinnati and forget about Aunt Aretha and her run-down house?

Because she was here in Copper Canyon, Idaho, to collect her inheritance, that's why, and she wasn't going to let a setting straight out of *Psycho* scare her into forfeiting it. If this was the house her great-aunt had left her when she died a few weeks ago, it was probably going to be more bother than it was worth, but Aretha had been her deceased father's only living relative. Jodi had seen the woman once and that was eighteen years ago when she was six years old. She'd forgotten she even had a great-aunt in Idaho until he'd received the letter telling her Aretha had died and he, Jodi, was her sole heir.

The bequest had come as a stunning surprise, but if retha wanted her to have the property, the least she could o was accept it.

On closer inspection Jodi could see that the structure was s decrepit as she'd suspected. The faded brown paint was eathered and peeling, and both the porch and the wide taircase leading up to it were so dilapidated that they apeared unsafe.

She supposed it would be called a three-story house, alough in the style of many of these old homes, the loweilinged foundation floor was actually the storage space, nd the second and third stories were living quarters.

Taking a deep breath she made her way carefully up the en shaky steps to the covered porch where she was at least ut of the rain. On the wall beside the door she found the ouse number, 940, and was forced to admit that this was e place she was looking for. But did she really want to o inside?

No, she didn't, but surely that would be better than wanering around in the storm. Rummaging in her purse she ame up with the key the executor had sent. But when she pened the screen door she saw at once that the lock on e heavy old oak one behind it had been smashed and was tanding ajar.

Someone had broken in! Minutes ago or weeks? Were ey still in there? There was no car near it other than her wn, and she hadn't seen anybody hanging around as she rove up. Nobody in their right mind would be out in this eather. On the other hand, they might be seeking refuge nside!

Gingerly she put out a trembling hand and pushed the oor wide open, then gasped. Although the tattered roller linds were pulled and the dense brush and trees further immed the light, she could see that the inside was a shambles. Furniture was overturned, drawers pulled out and personal papers and any other movable objects were scattered around the living room.

Someone had torn this room—and probably the whole place—apart, and Jodi was no Nancy Drew. She turned and ran down the steps. No way was she going in there alone! She'd let the police handle it.

Across town at the Copper Canyon Police Department, Chief Richard McBride put down the telephone and sighed. Dear old Addie Rolf. She had to be in her nineties and still lived alone in the house where she'd been born and raised, but somewhere along the way her slightly scrambled mind had come up with the idea that it was part of the duties of the police department to run errands for her.

He'd known her all his life, and shortly after he came back to Copper Canyon to take on the job of police chief she'd fallen and hurt her leg. He'd responded to the 911 call and driven her to the hospital. Since she had no family he'd stayed with her while they patched her up, then he'd taken her home and made arrangements with social services to have someone come in and care for her until she could get around again.

Rick had stopped in from time to time to make sure she was okay and do some grocery shopping for her, and ever since then she'd called him when she needed an errand run. She was so grateful and so effusive in her thanks that he hadn't had the heart to turn her down, so he'd recruited a few volunteers from among the officers and staff and the force had become her private delivery service.

Pushing aside the reports he'd been reading, he left his office and went out into the main room in search of a patsy…uh, volunteer. There were two officers chatting with the dispatcher at her desk. Copper Canyon wasn't exactly the crime capital of the world, and when the officers weren't chasing down teenage joyriders or locking up unruly drunks or an occasional drug dealer they sometimes had trouble keeping busy.

"Which one of you guys wants to pick up some groceries and run them over to Addie?" he asked.

"Excuse me, Chief, but I'd like to point out that I'm not a 'guy,'" said Evelyn Williams, the dispatcher.

Rick chuckled. "Yes, ma'am, correction noted. Now, who wants to do our good deed for the day?"

Both male officers groaned and stood. "We'll do it," one of them said. "We just got a call about a tree limb that was snapped by the wind and is in danger of falling on a house. We'll run the errand after we check that out."

"Yeah, well, call the utility company and tell them to check on it, too. Don't want it falling across any hot lines."

"Will do," the other officer promised as the two of them walked out.

Rick had just started back to his office when he heard the door open again, and he turned to see an attractive young woman approaching the counter that separated the work area from the general public. She was all bundled up in a hooded parka, but once she'd pushed the hood back to reveal the delicate bone structure of her face and the near perfect symmetry of her features, he knew he'd never seen her before. He also knew he'd like to see her again, often.

That meant that she probably didn't live in the area. He'd been born and brought up here as well as being chief of police for the past three years, and he knew everyone for miles around, both criminal and law abiding. No way would he have forgotten that rich auburn hair and those deep set blue eyes, not to mention the long slender legs and tantalizingly rounded hips that her clinging wet blue jeans revealed below her parka.

"Officer, I want to report a...a burglary," she said breathlessly, her face flushed. "Someone broke into my house and ransacked it—"

"*Your* house?" he interrupted, surprised. "Do you live here?"

He didn't see how a woman as spectacular looking as she was could come to town and set up residence without causing something of a sensation.

"No, I... That is, the house belonged to my great-aunt, but now she's dead and—"

Rick opened the swinging gate on the counter and stood back. "Please come in here and we'll fill out a report," he said softly, trying to calm her down enough so she could tell him accurately whatever it was that had upset her.

She did as he requested and he seated her at one of the desks, then walked around to the opposite side and put out his hand. "I'm Richard McBride, and you are—"

"Jodi Hopkins," she said and put her hand in his. Hers was small and soft, but she had a firm grip that led him to suspect she was usually independent and not in the habit of running to the police or anyone else to solve her problems. Something fairly serious must have happened.

Reluctantly he released her hand and sat down across from her where he could type on the computer. "May I call you Jodi?" he asked. He liked to get on a first name basis with people who had been victimized. It helped to put them at ease.

"Please do," she answered.

"And I'm Rick. Now, first I'll need your full name, and the address of the house that has been broken into."

She seemed to relax a little. "My name is Jodi Patricia Hopkins, and the address is 940 Red Robin Lane."

That jolted him. "Was your aunt Aretha Coldwell?" he blurted.

She looked somewhat taken aback. "Yes. Did you know her?"

"Of course I knew her. Everybody in town knew her, but I didn't know she had any living relatives."

"Only me," she told him, "and I didn't remember that

I had an aunt—great-aunt, actually—until I was notified of her death.''

Rick held up his hand. ''Just a minute, please,'' he said and turned to the dispatcher. ''Evelyn, contact those two officers who just left and reroute them to the Coldwell house on Red Robin Lane,'' he ordered. ''Tell them it's a possible burglary in progress.''

''Yes, sir,'' the dispatcher said and spoke into her microphone while Rick returned his attention to Jodi.

''They'll take care of it,'' he assured her. ''Now, I'll need your present address and telephone number, both home and business.''

She seemed to relax a little. ''My address is 1531 Yellow Brick Road, Cincinnati, Ohio—''

His eyebrows arched incredulously. ''Yellow Brick Road?''

She laughed. A soft tinkling sound that matched the musical tone of her voice and sent prickles down his spine. ''I'm afraid so. I live in a subdivision that has streets named after characters and places in *The Wizard of Oz*. It's no weirder, though, than Red Robin Lane, which is right here in Copper Canyon.''

''Touché,'' he said with a grin. ''Your phone numbers?''

She gave them to him. ''I'm a preschool teacher and I work at the Tots 'n' Toddlers nursery school.''

His stomach sank but he plowed on. ''Like kids, do you?''

She smiled again. ''I love them. Someday I hope to have a houseful of my own.''

He almost groaned aloud. Why was it that the women who appealed to him were always the maternal types who couldn't wait to make babies? The only interest they had in husbands was someone to father their kids.

''Okay, now tell me why you're here in Idaho and what happened to bring you to the police station.'' He settled back in his chair and vowed to keep his distance and not to let this appealing young woman get to him on a personal basis.

"Well," she began haltingly, "after I was notified of Aunt Aretha's death and that I was her sole heir, I arranged to take a leave of absence from the preschool and left Cincinnati to drive to Copper Canyon and claim the estate. I only arrived here within the hour and drove directly to the address her executor, a man named Harlan Lowery, had given me. Do you know Mr. Lowery?"

He nodded. "Oh, sure, he's vice president of the First National Bank here in town."

She shifted uneasily in her chair. "I...I just wanted to see the house I'd inherited before I contacted him, but when I finally found it I..."

Her voice caught and she twisted her hands in her lap. "Officer McBride, I can't believe that my aunt lived in that...that dreadful place...."

Rick interrupted. "You're going to call me Rick, remember, Jodi? And my official title is Chief McBride."

Her eyes widened with disbelief. "You're the chief of police?"

He laughed. "You sound surprised. Actually, I'm a damn good chief if I do say so—"

"No, no, it's not that," she protested. "It's just that you're so young. Police chiefs are usually older men."

He continued to chuckle. "I'm thirty-three and studied police science in college before entering the academy. Don't worry, I'm well qualified, but bringing up the subject of age reminds me that I forgot to ask you yours."

Her lovely face flushed with embarrassment. "Please believe me, I wasn't questioning your qualifications. I'm twenty-four years old, and I studied early childhood education in college."

He typed the information into the computer. "Am I right in assuming you're not married? That is, you're not wearing a wedding ring."

She looked down at her hands. "No, I'm not married." She looked pointedly at his third finger on his left hand, apparently curious but too polite to ask.

That both surprised and pleased him. She was noticing small, personal things about him, too. Was it possible she was as interested in him as he was in her?

He shook his head. "I'm not married, either. Never have been. After college I worked for the Detroit police department for six years, and believe me, a big-city P.D. is no place for a family man, although most of the officers are. It's a jungle out there on the streets."

His good sense finally caught up with his wagging tongue, and he shut his mouth. All she'd asked was whether or not he was married. She wasn't interested in a discourse on why he wasn't.

Then she surprised him again by asking, "But you're not working the streets of Detroit anymore. There's not much crime in Copper Canyon, is there?"

He could spend all afternoon happily visiting with her, but she was here to report a crime and he'd better get on with it.

"No, there's not," he said, "but apparently one has been committed quite recently. Tell me what happened when you got to your aunt's house."

Jodi had been discreetly studying Officer Richard McBride while they talked. It would have been difficult not to. He was a real hunk! Tall, with short blond hair and inquisitive brown eyes that seemed to bore into her very soul. As if that weren't enough he had bulging muscles that rippled right through the light blue shirt of his uniform and made her itch to touch them.

Only he wasn't just an officer. He was the chief of police in this cozy little foothills village.

She described her experience at the house. "I turned and ran," she concluded. "I...I don't suppose there was any real danger. I didn't hear or see anybody around, but after living all my life in a big city, I'm conditioned to get help and let the police investigate crime. There are just too many people with guns and no hesitation about using them on the city streets."

"You did exactly right," he assured her. "Even small towns have their share of crazies these days. I'll go out there and take a look for myself. You stay here where it's warm and dry—"

"No, please," she interrupted. "I want to go with you. I promise I won't get in the way, but I'd like to have someone with me when I go through the house. It...it's so spooky." She shivered involuntarily and knew she was behaving like a wimp.

He looked at her and apparently understood her fear. "It's not a matter of you getting in *my* way," he said softly. "I don't want you in harm's way. If someone is burglarizing the place he'll very likely have a gun, too."

"I—I can drive my own car..." she stammered.

"No," he said firmly as he pushed back his chair and stood. "If you're going I want you with me where I can keep an eye on you."

She stood, too, and smiled. "Thank you. I promise I won't be a bother."

He grabbed a shiny dark blue waterproof jacket and matching cap off the rack by the door and put them on, then took her arm and together they walked outside and ran through the wind and rain to the old black-and-white police car parked in front of the building.

It wasn't a very long ride, and on the way Rick gave her instructions. "The two officers I sent over will be there, but I want you to stay in the car until I take a look around and make sure everything's under control. That's a non-negotiable order and I expect you to obey, understand?"

She nodded her head. "That's fine with me, but you will go through the place again with me, won't you?"

He grinned. "Sure I will. Can you tell me exactly how long the house has been empty?"

"No, I'm sorry, I have no idea. I understand my aunt died in the hospital, but I don't know how long she was there. Actually, I don't know anything about her, but surely Mr. Lowery will have more information."

"We'll go talk to him as soon as we're finished here," Rick said as he slowed down and pulled the car over to the curb.

He opened the door and got out, then turned to face her again. "Now stay in the car, hear? As soon as I'm sure it's safe I'll come back and get you."

She nodded, and he sprinted down the street and disappeared into the tangle of foliage that surrounded the house.

Jodi sat rooted to the seat, her eyes and ears straining for the sights and sounds of a commotion, but the windshield and windows quickly fogged over so she could see nothing. The only sound was of tree branches whipping in the wind and raindrops beating on the roof of the car.

The strain of waiting seemed to go on forever. Her raw nerves were screaming when suddenly the door opened!

She jumped and yelped before she saw Rick standing in the open doorway beside her.

"It's okay, Jodi, it's just me," he said anxiously. "I'm sorry, I didn't mean to scare you. I've sent the officers back to the station. They didn't find anybody in the house, but you're right, it's been ransacked. Do you still want to take the tour?"

She felt the flush of embarrassment that darkened her complexion, and cleared her throat. "I'm the one who's sorry. I don't know what's gotten into me. I'm usually not so easily scared. It must be the combination of the storm and the spooky old house."

She turned in her seat and put her feet on the curb. "I definitely do want to take the tour. Maybe you can fill me in on what I'm looking at. As I told you, I didn't know

Aunt Aretha at all, so I don't know what kind of person she was."

Rick helped her out of the car. "Your aunt was a very private person," he told her as they scurried through the wet gale. "She never socialized much, and after her husband died about ten years ago she became more and more reclusive, until finally she got so she didn't go out of the house at all. Even had her groceries delivered."

They turned into the thicket that overran the property and made their way up the stairs. "For the past two or three years she spent all her time alone in this big empty house."

Rick took the flashlight off his belt and pushed open the front door, then preceded her inside. "I rolled up the blinds, but it's still pretty dim in here. Take my hand and watch that you don't stumble over the mess on the floor."

She put her hand in his, and his was big, and strong, and rough with calluses. He snapped on his flashlight and shone it around the room. The devastation was every bit as bad as her first glimpse had convinced her it was.

He led her around the downstairs which consisted of a living room, dining room, kitchen, parlor and bathroom. All were high ceilinged, large and grimy as well as messy. There were years' worth of newspapers and magazines stacked all over the house, and the dirt was deeply ingrained. Aunt Aretha hadn't scrubbed it or had it scrubbed in years! It even smelled of mildew and garbage.

"Are you sure Aunt Aretha lived in this pigsty?" Jodi asked incredulously.

"I'm afraid so," he said. "Long ago she made it plain that she wanted to be left alone, so people and agencies stopped offering her help. She must have called the doctor at the last, though, since she died in the hospital."

They explored the four bedrooms and bath upstairs, which were all in as bad shape as the downstairs, and Jodi's plan to stay in the house while she was here came to a screeching halt. No way was she going to spend any more time than she had to in this place!

"Did you check the ground floor?" she asked as they prepared to leave.

"Yeah. There's nothing there but discarded furniture and boxes of junk. I looked around to make sure nobody was hiding there, but I didn't disturb anything. You're not going to stay here, are you?"

She shuddered. "Heavens, no! I'd intended to, but not after I saw it. Is there a hotel or motel in town where I can get a room?"

"We'll find something. Meanwhile you'd better have that lock fixed. Thank God, none of the windows were broken."

Once more they braved the storm to run to the car.

Jodi was thoroughly chilled and she continued to shiver even after the heater was turned on. Her jeans were wet as were her shoes and her feet inside them, and water ran off her parka and hood.

Rick glanced at her and commented, "You're soaking wet. We're going back to the station to pick up your luggage and find a place for you to take a hot shower and get into dry clothes before we go over to the bank to talk to Lowery."

It didn't sound as if he was giving her a choice, but she didn't protest. All she could think of was getting warm again.

Back at the police station he took her luggage from the trunk of her car and put it into his, then climbed back in the driver's seat. "You're welcome to shower and change at my house," he said as he started the car, "or if you'd rather, I can take you to my parents' home. I'm pretty sure Mom will be there."

Jodi hesitated. "I—I don't like to bother your parents," she stammered. "Besides, you're the police chief. I should be safe with you. If I can't trust you, then who can I trust?"

He chuckled. "Don't forget, I'm also a male. You'd better be careful about trusting any of us too far."

She smiled. "Do I need to worry?"

He sobered and shook his head. "No. I can control my baser instincts, but if it will make you feel better, I'll drop you off at home and then come back here for half an hour or so and catch up on some of my work."

"I'm being an awful nuisance," she murmured.

He pulled the car away from the curb. "Not at all, I really do need to make some phone calls. Will forty-five minutes give you enough time?"

Jodi assured him that it would, and a short while later they pulled into the driveway of a cheerful yellow cottage on a pretty street that looked like Red Robin Lane should have but instead was called Cobblestone Terrace, although there wasn't a cobblestone or a terrace in sight.

The trees and bushes were rapidly losing their foliage in the October chill, but she could see that they would be lush in the spring and summer. Inside was the usual two-bedroom floor plan with a sliding glass door in the living room that led onto a redwood deck. The house was built on the side of a hill, and the deck looked out over the towering mountains in the background.

"You have a lovely home," Jodi said appreciatively.

It was strictly a bachelor pad with solid wood and leather furniture, earthen-colored walls and decor, and colorful though rugged landscapes and animal oil paintings on the walls. It looked comfortable, lived-in and private. A place where a hard working man could come at the end of the day and either relax or entertain at his own pace.

"It suits me," Rick said as he strode ahead of her with her suitcase and cosmetic bag. "You can use the master bath and bedroom. There are towels in the hall closet and shampoo and stuff in the bathroom cupboard. Feel free to use anything you need."

They'd reached the bedroom and he put the suitcase on

the expensive-looking heavy quilted orange-and-brown spread atop the king-sized bed. Jodi opened her mouth to protest, but he was already striding out of the room.

"I'll be back in three quarters of an hour," he said over his shoulder as he walked out the door and shut it behind him.

Chapter Two

The First National Bank turned out to be a two story red-brick building on the corner of the second block of Main Street. When Jodi stepped out of the police car she noticed that catty-corner across the street was a gray building with a large sign on the front that read Citizens Bank. She chuckled with amusement. "Why are this town's two banks just across the street from each other?" she asked Rick as he joined her on the sidewalk.

He grinned. "Damned if I know. Citizens was there first, though. It was a fixture in town before First National was built."

In the hour it had taken Jodi to shower and change, the rain had stopped and the wind had tamed down to a breeze. Together they entered the bank, passing by the tellers' cages to the back of the room where a middle aged woman sat at a desk that was situated between two doors. "Afternoon, Vera," Rick said pleasantly as the woman looked up. "Any chance we can talk to Harlan? If he's not too busy, that is."

Vera smiled. "Sure, Chief, he's in his office. Go on in."

Rick thanked her and ushered Jodi to the first door. It was unlatched and he pushed it open to reveal a man sitting behind a desk. "Hi, Harlan. Got something I need to talk to you about. Can you spare a minute?"

The man looked up. "Sure, Rick, come on in."

They walked into the office. It was small but tastefully furnished and neat. The man behind the desk stood and looked at Jodi with both curiosity and admiration. She was glad she'd changed into a dress after her shower, and that her tan Burberry raincoat, which she'd splurged on a couple of years before, kept her warm and dry.

"Harlan," Rick said, "I'd like you to meet Jodi Hopkins, from Cincinnati. She's Aretha Coldwell's great-niece, and she says you're the executor of Aretha's estate."

So this was the man she'd been conversing with via long-distance since her aunt's death. He didn't look like a big-city banker, but he wasn't a hick, either. He wore a gray suit with a white shirt and blue patterned tie, and his dark hair lightly sprinkled with white was starting to recede.

He blinked, but thick, dark-framed glasses made it difficult for Jodi to tell whether his eyes were amber or hazel.

She put out her hand and smiled. "I'm glad to meet you, Mr. Lowery. I would have been here sooner, but I had to stop off at the police station to report a break-in at Aunt Aretha's house."

She'd obviously surprised him, but it didn't take him long to recoup. He took her hand and shook it. "Jodi, you should have let me know you were coming. I didn't expect you until sometime next week. Please, sit down."

Releasing her hand he looked at Rick. "What's this about a break-in?"

They all took seats and Rick answered. "Someone broke the lock on the empty Coldwell house and trashed the place. Can you tell me how long it's been empty? Wasn't somebody supposed to be watching it?"

The questions were not accusations but they were firm,

and Harlan bristled. "Now look here, I'm not responsible for that house. You know its reputation. Usually people can't even be coaxed into going near it."

That captured Jodi's full attention. "What do you mean, its reputation? What reputation, and why do people avoid it?"

"If you've seen the place already you must know what I'm talking about." He sounded annoyed. "Aretha never was very sociable, and after her husband died ten years ago she just holed up in that old house and vegetated. Let the place fall apart around her. It finally got so disreputable that people started calling it the haunted house. Pretty soon everyone got to thinking it was, and that Aretha was some kind of witch."

Jodi winced. "Wasn't anyone concerned about her strange behavior?" Her tone was more accusatory than she'd intended.

"Sure they were at first," he said huffily, "but she let it be known in no uncertain terms that she didn't want either visitors or help. As far as I know the only people allowed on her property for the past several years were the mailman and the delivery boy from the one grocery store that still delivers."

"But she must have needed money—"

"All her financial transactions were done by mail," Harlan interrupted. "Her investments were managed by the bank so as long as she paid her bills on time, everyone assumed she was all right and didn't bother her. After all, she did have a right to privacy."

Jodi sighed. "Yes, I suppose she did, but how come she was in the hospital when she died? I gather she didn't receive regular medical checkups."

"No, she didn't, and when she called Dr. Sam about two weeks ago, said she was sick and asked him to make a house call, he tore right over there figuring something was wrong. He found her only barely conscious and immediately called for an ambulance to take her to the hospital. She died the following day of pneumonia and various other health problems that had been long neglected.''

Rick spoke then. ''So she occupied the house right up to the day before she died?''

Harlan nodded. ''That's right. The bank is actually the executor of her estate, and when we heard about her death I was appointed to handle it. I went over and locked the house up, then called Ms. Hopkins to notify her.''

''The preschool found a substitute teacher more quickly than I thought they would,'' Jodi explained. ''That's why I was able to get away sooner than anticipated. I'd planned to stay at the house so I drove by there first to leave my suitcases and stuff, but that was before I saw it.''

She shuddered and glared at him. ''You didn't tell me it was such a ruin.''

He shifted uncomfortably. ''Didn't see any need to. I didn't spell out any of the details of your aunt's estate on the phone. You said you'd come as soon as you could get away so I didn't see any reason to go into it twice. I expected you to let me know when you were arriving, though.'' He glared back at her.

It occurred to Jodi that it wasn't very smart to antagonize her aunt's executor. Especially this one who seemed to take offense easily. He'd informed her that Aretha's estate was a sizable one, so it would probably take a while to settle. She was already at a disadvantage, living out of state and all. This man could make things even more difficult if he got teed off.

Besides, she really should have let him know ahead of time when she'd be showing up.

She tamped down her resentment and smiled. ''I'm sorry I was so thoughtless. I noticed a motel on the highway as I was coming into town. Can you recommend it?'' She looked from Harlan to Rick.

They both nodded. "Yeah," Harlan said, "it's the newest one around here."

"I've heard good things about it," Rick agreed.

"Then I'll stay there," she decided aloud. "Now, when can we get together, Mr. Lowery, and start getting this estate settled?"

Rick pushed his chair back and rose. "I'll leave you two to discuss business while I make a phone call. I'll wait for you outside, Jodi."

A few minutes later she found him talking to the secretary, Vera, at her desk. He introduced the two women and they chatted for a few minutes, then she and Rick got into the police car and drove slowly up the street.

"About finding you a place to stay while you're here," he said. "I phoned my mother and explained your problem. She said you'd be welcome to stay with Dad and her. They've got extra bedrooms now that all their kids are grown."

Jodi blinked. "Stay with your parents? But I wouldn't think of imposing—"

"You wouldn't be imposing," he assured her. "I didn't ask her to let you stay there, she invited you before I could. Besides, you're sort of a shirttail relation. Your aunt's husband and my dad were second cousins."

"But—"

"No, really, they'd love to have you. They were used to a houseful of rowdy kids who kept life lively, but now they wander around in that big place all alone. It will be good for them, and a lot better for you than a lonely motel room where you'd have to eat all your meals out. At least let me take you over and introduce you to them."

Jodi's mind was in a whirl. Why would his parents want a stranger in their nice, peaceful home? There was no true relationship between her and Rick's family.

"How many, uh, siblings do you have?" she asked.

"Two brothers and a sister. My older brother, Nathan,

is thirty-five, married with one son and is a career navy man. Jessica is twenty-eight, married, has two little girls and lives in Boise, and Barry's eighteen and a freshman at Idaho U."

He chuckled. "Dad and Mom really miss Barry. He's their baby, and this is his first time away from home. They'll be delighted to have someone to fuss over again."

Jodi wasn't so sure about that, but the offer was tempting. The idea of spending a week or two in a dreary motel room where she couldn't even fix a meal for herself was depressing.

"Well, I... If you're sure..." she stammered. "I'd like to talk to your mom about it."

Rick grinned. "You'll like her. Dad, too. You and he have a lot in common. You're both into education. Dad's superintendent of all the county schools."

Jodi's eyes widened with surprise. "He is! That must be quite a job."

Rick turned off Main Street and headed east. "Well, yes, he keeps plenty busy."

After another turn Rick stopped the car in front of a large two-story house in an upper-class neighborhood of old but well-preserved homes. They were set on spacious lots with thick lawns and massive trees that Jodi knew must be beautiful in the spring, summer and early fall when they were all leafed out and green.

The McBride home was beige with brown trim, and it had a bay window that jutted out at the front. "It's lovely," Jodi exclaimed.

"Comfortable, too," Rick said. "It was a great place to grow up in. It's too big for Dad and Mom now, but they'd never sell it. Too many happy memories."

"Does your mother work?" Jodi asked as she opened her door and got out.

He joined her on the sidewalk. "No, not since her first

baby was born. She was a secretary at the utility company before that, but she quit when they started their family."

They climbed the few steps to the porch, and Rick rang the doorbell, then opened the door without waiting. A matronly woman dressed in black slacks and a billowing black-and-white shirt met them in the good-sized entry hall. Her blond hair was devoid of gray, and she greeted them with a big smile and a sparkle in her sky blue eyes.

"Come on in," she said cheerfully, then turned her attention to Jodi. "You're Jodi, right? Rick called about you. I'm Dorothy. Let me have your coats and I'll put them in the closet."

There was a staircase that went up the wall to their right, with a closet beneath it. She opened the door and hung up their wraps.

"The coffeepot's on and I just finished baking cookies, so why don't we sit at the table in the kitchen." Jodi didn't have a chance to say anything before the other woman turned and opened the door straight ahead of them that led into a big old-fashioned kitchen.

It was warm, and homey, and smelled of perking coffee and of vanilla and cinnamon. Jodi's mouth began to water, and she told herself that Rick and his mother were going to have to throw her out if they wanted to get rid of her. No way was she leaving voluntarily.

"Oh, it smells so good in here," she said on a sigh, "and this is the first time I've been warm all day."

"I'll bet you haven't eaten all day, either, have you?"

Now that Jodi thought of it, she hadn't, and she looked at her watch. It was after three o'clock! "Well, I..." she paused thinking. "I had coffee and a piece of toast at about six this morning, but—"

"You just sit right down there at the table," Dorothy insisted, "and I'll fix you a sandwich to go with the cookies and coffee. That should get you through until supper."

"But, Mrs. McBride," Jodi protested, "I don't want to be a bother—"

"Call me Dorothy. We don't stand on formality around here. Everyone in Copper Canyon is on a first-name basis." She'd already gathered up the ingredients and was fixing a ham sandwich. "I don't suppose Richard's had lunch yet, either, have you?" she asked as she glanced at Rick.

He grinned. "You suppose right, Ma. How about fixing me one of those, too?"

He seated Jodi at the table on one side of the kitchen, then took mugs from the cupboard, unplugged the coffee-pot, which had stopped perking, and poured coffee for the two of them. "Do you want some, too, Mom?"

"No, thanks, I had two cups for lunch," she answered.

"You'd better come for supper, too," she said, still addressing Rick. "Otherwise you won't have a decent meal all day."

"Yes, ma'am," Rick answered happily and winked at Jodi.

"Mrs. McBride...uh, Dorothy," Jodi corrected herself. "Rick says you've invited me to stay with you and Mr. McBride while I'm in town, but I don't want to impose—"

"You're not imposing," Dorothy interrupted. "We'd love to have you, and it doesn't make sense for you to stay alone in a motel when we have three spare bedrooms."

Jodi saw no reason not to believe her. "That's very nice of you, and I accept with pleasure, but you won't have to feed me. I can eat out—"

Dorothy put the sandwiches on plates and sliced them in two crosswise. "Nonsense. I have to fix meals for Shawn and me—it's no bother to cook for one more. You're also welcome to use the kitchen between meals anytime you like."

Jodi was overcome with gratitude for this woman's generosity. "I...I don't know what to say..."

"*Yes* will do nicely," Dorothy said as she picked up the

plates and carried them to the table. She'd added potato chips, and the cookies she'd promised were already there, heaped on a crystal tray.

"*Yes* is what I want to say," Jodi admitted, "but if I do I will, of course, pay room and board."

Dorothy sat down and frowned as she drew in her breath, then nodded. "All right, if you'll feel more comfortable with that arrangement, but understand, it's not necessary."

Jodi relaxed and smiled. "I understand that it's not necessary to you, but it is to me. Okay?"

Dorothy smiled, too. "Now that that's settled, tell me about yourself. Richard says you're Aretha Coldwell's niece from Cincinnati, Ohio. I'm so sorry about your aunt's death, and the vandalism of her home. She was my husband's distant cousin by marriage, but we hadn't seen her in years. She kept to herself and seldom went out."

"She was my great-aunt, actually," Jodi said. "My grandfather Hopkins's sister, and I didn't know her at all. The only time I ever saw her was at my father's funeral, and I was only six at the time. According to my mother, Aretha was estranged from the rest of Dad's family, and after his death none of us ever saw or heard from her again."

"What a tragic waste," Dorothy murmured. "And what about your mother? Do you live with her?"

Jodi realized that Rick's mother wasn't prying, she was just interested. "Oh, no," she answered. "Mom married Paul Osborn when I was eight and he moved into our house. We all lived together until my first year of college, when Dad's employer transferred him to Atlanta. I didn't want to leave Cincinnati, so Mom and Dad let me stay on in the house instead of selling it. I pay them rent, which covers the taxes, upkeep and incidentals."

Dorothy picked up a cookie and looked at it. "I notice you call your stepfather Dad."

Jodi nodded. "He is my dad. I only vaguely remember

my birth father, but Paul helped raise me and has been my dad in every sense of the word. I love him dearly."

Dorothy's soft blue eyes misted, and she reached over to pat Jodi's hand. "That's so sweet. Your Paul is a lucky dad."

Jodi was feeling a little misty-eyed, too. "No, I'm a lucky daughter."

Later that evening Jodi, Rick, Dorothy and Rick's dad, Shawn, sat around the kitchen table finishing up their supper. It was an informal family setting, and Jodi felt right at home.

Shawn McBride was every bit as friendly and welcoming as Dorothy had been. His black hair was liberally salted with gray, but that was the only part of him that had succumbed to age, and even it looked premature. He was a big man, almost as big as his son, and the muscles under his shirt left no doubt about his strength.

His deep blue eyes sparkled as he and Jodi discussed their mutual interest in education. "Are you planning to make a career of working with preschool children," he asked her, "or will you eventually go back to school and get a credential to teach in the higher grades?"

People often asked her that so she wasn't taken by surprise. "I'm not sure. I love babies and toddlers, and I hope to have several of my own. Ideally, when that happens I'll stay home and take care of them, at least until the youngest is in school."

She laughed. "If, by then, I'm tired of changing diapers and wiping pureed food off little chins I'll get my credential to teach at another grade level, but I suspect that I'll always be most happy with the little ones."

Rick had that familiar sinking feeling as he listened to Jodi speak so eagerly of the family she expected to have, but this time it was stronger and more painful than ever before. He'd been watching her as she and his dad talked.

For that matter he'd been watching her all through supper. She was such a joy to look at that it was difficult for him to take his eyes off her. She positively glowed with good health and enthusiasm. Her cheeks were naturally pink and so were her full, tempting lips.

He was no novice with women, and he'd learned to recognize makeup when they wore it. He'd bet all he had that she wasn't wearing any. Her complexion was unblemished and looked smooth as a baby's tender skin. His fingers itched to touch it, to feel its softness and its warmth—

Abruptly he pulled his thoughts away from that pit of enticement. He was already much too far into it. He never should have suggested that she stay with his parents. He'd known it at the time but went ahead and did it, anyway. Now he wouldn't be able to avoid her.

Not that he wanted to. If things were different he'd court her with all the respect and passion that was rapidly building up inside him. But things weren't different, and he knew he could never be anything to her but the friendly police chief.

So why in hell had he brought her home to Mom and Dad!

He shifted in his chair in an effort to dislodge his thoughts, but his gaze settled on Jodi's hands as she gestured expressively with them. They were small but strong. He knew that from shaking hands with her, but they were also white and dainty with pink manicured nails that were neither too short or too long. She wouldn't accidentally scratch one of her small charges, but she could draw lines and circles on a man's bare back with them and make him moan with pleasure.

He almost groaned aloud as once more he wrestled with his runaway thoughts. Dammit, it was time for him to get out of here before he did or said something he'd regret.

Pushing back his chair he stood. "If you'll excuse me, I

still have work to do at the station before I can call it a day.''

He went around the table and leaned down to kiss his mother's cheek. ''Thanks for the supper, Mom. You still make the best roast beef hash I ever tasted.''

Dorothy put her hand up and patted her son's cheek. ''You know you're welcome to drop in for a meal anytime. And thank you for bringing Jodi to us. It'll be good to have a young person in the house again.''

Jodi surprised him then by pushing back her chair and standing, too. ''Do you mind if I walk to the door with you?'' she asked shyly.

Mind? He'd spent the past five minutes fighting down the urge to *ask* her to come with him.

He didn't answer her but smiled, then took her hand. ''Bye, Dad,'' he said over his shoulder and headed out the door into the reception hall, then closed it firmly behind them.

At the front door she removed her hand from his, then turned and tilted her head up to face him. ''Rick,'' she said softly, ''I don't know how I can ever thank you for talking your parents into letting me stay here with them—''

He put one finger across her lips and found that they were as tempting to the touch as they looked. ''I didn't 'talk them' into anything, Jodi,'' he said huskily. ''Not that I wouldn't have if Mom hadn't suggested it first.''

He stroked the finger slowly around her lips, and her small puff of breath on his sensitized flesh made his whole hand and arm tingle.

''Will you be seeing Lowery tomorrow?'' He was only vaguely aware of what he was saying.

''Yes,'' she said against his finger, and he removed it and took her hand in his. ''I have an appointment for ten o'clock in the morning. We're going to explore the house and its contents.''

"Let me know if you have any trouble, hear?" He was aware of the quiver in his tone.

She looked straight into his eyes. Her big blue ones were soft and shimmering. "Will you...that is, would you have time to go with us?" Her lips trembled and he wondered how he was ever going to force himself to resist their sweet but unintended invitation. He was acutely aware that if he lowered his head to her upturned face he could easily capture her mouth with his own. Just the thought of that made him shiver, and he knew he was dangerously close to losing what little self-control he had left.

"I...I'll make time," he whispered, and with a last burst of effort he released her hand, then stroked her cheek with the back of his fingers. "Good night, Jodi. I'll meet you and Harlan at your house at ten-thirty in the morning."

He quickly opened the door and walked out, closing it softly behind him.

Chapter Three

Jodi awakened slowly the following morning, but she wasn't a bit disoriented when she finally opened her eyes in the unfamiliar bedroom. She knew exactly where she was, and she remembered everything that had happened yesterday. It had been much too memorable to forget.

Especially the evening! She'd never been so strongly attracted to a man, and certainly not as quickly, as she was to Rick McBride. She felt a happy tingle as she remembered his leave-taking. He'd felt the enticement, too. She couldn't have been mistaken about that. It took two to generate that much magnetism, even though he had broken the tender scene off rather abruptly.

She glanced around the room. Dorothy had told her it used to be her daughter Jessica's when she was growing up, and it still looked like a young girl's domain with its pink flounces and frills. Dorothy said Jess's small daughters shared it and the twin beds now when they visited.

Lucky children, both the grandkids and the adult sons and daughter. Being a part of Shawn and Dorothy McBride's family must have been pure heaven.

Not that Jodi's own childhood had been unhappy. It hadn't. She'd had loving parents and a comfortable amount of security, but she'd been lonely. As an only child she'd missed the camaraderie of brothers and sisters. That was one reason she wanted a big family of her own. That is, if she ever found a man qualified to father those children.

So far she hadn't met one she wanted to spend the rest of her life with, and that's what marriage was to her. A lifetime commitment. Her husband must want babies as much as she did, and be willing to do whatever it took to forge a loving family union that could never be ripped apart.

On the other hand, given time, she suspected that Richard McBride could step quite comfortably into that role.

But she didn't have time. Her stay in Copper Canyon would be short, and then she'd go back to Cincinnati where she had a job she loved, a comfortable home she could afford and friends she'd grown up with. She wasn't about to gamble all that on the possibility of a relationship that might go nowhere, with a small-town police chief who lived halfway across the country and was probably no more eager to gamble on her.

A glance at her watch told her it was eight-thirty, and she jumped out of bed and reached for her suitcase. She had just an hour and a half to shower, unpack her clothes, dress, grab a cup of coffee and get to the bank in time for her appointment with Harlan Lowery.

With a lot of hurry and a little luck she got to the office on time and was ushered in by Vera. "Well, Jodi," Lowery said as his gaze roamed over her much as it had yesterday. It made her skin crawl. "I see you dressed appropriately for searching through that cluttered old house."

She was wearing jeans and a navy blue sweatshirt with white thick-soled sneakers and her quilted parka that she'd run through Dorothy's clothes dryer last night.

He was dressed in cotton slacks and a plaid flannel shirt.

He looked different from the haughty banker of the day before, but his manner was just as imperious.

"Rick walked me through it yesterday so I knew what to expect," she told him coolly.

"I understand you're staying with Rick's parents." His tone was laced with a touch of insinuation, startling Jodi speechless for a moment. Just what was he implying?

"How...how did you know that?" she finally managed to ask.

He shrugged. "This is a small town, word gets around pretty fast. Especially when a beautiful young woman is involved. You'd better watch your step if you don't want people to talk. Now, I have a couple of forms for you to fill out, then we'll go over there." He pushed several sheets of paper across the desk at her and handed her a pen.

Jodi was furious at his thinly veiled assertion that she was making a play for Rick by staying with his parents, but she wasn't going to let Harlan know his little dart had hit its mark. She picked up the pen and one of the papers. "Oh, by the way," she said sweetly, "Rick is going to meet us there at ten-thirty."

Harlan didn't look pleased. "What on earth for? This isn't a police matter."

"It most certainly is," she responded. "Don't forget the place was broken into and ransacked. Someone must have been looking for something. I don't want to run into a stash of coke in the basement or a field of marijuana among the overgrown weeds in that jungle of a yard, and I'd really hate to stumble over a dead body without a lawman present. I asked Rick to come with us and he said he would."

She eyed Harlan suspiciously. "I assumed you'd have no objections?" Her tone made it plain that he'd better not have.

"No, no, of course not." He waved his hand in a dismissive manner. "But don't you think you're overreacting?

You're not in the big city now. We don't have murderers and drug dealers here."

She saw the flush of anger that stained his face and wondered if he was really that naive. She doubted it. She'd dealt with men like him before. He'd probably been hoping for a little hanky-panky among the ruins and didn't welcome a third party.

"There are drug dealers and homicides in every town," she informed him, "and I'm sure Copper Canyon is no exception."

He glared at her, then excused himself and went out of the office while she filled out the forms. A short time later they left to go to her aunt's house.

Jodi didn't take her car but rode with Harlan in his since they had more business to take care of back at his office when they finished their inspection.

"What do you plan to do with the property once the estate is settled?" he asked her as they neared their destination. "Surely you don't plan to live there."

She shook her head. "Oh, no, I have a comfortable life back in Cincinnati and have no desire to relocate. I'd expected to sell it, but now that I know it's supposed to be haunted that might be difficult."

"Very difficult indeed," he intoned, "but if you'd like I'll introduce you to Farley Finch, the town's real estate agent. He can unload it if anyone can."

That remark didn't exactly reassure her.

"Do you plan to stay here long?" he asked.

"No longer than it takes to sell the property and get the estate settled and closed."

He frowned. "Oh, it won't be necessary for you to wait around until the house is sold. The bulk of your inheritance is in stocks, bonds and CDs. Those can be gone over and transferred to you within a matter of days."

That intriguing remark caught her attention. Just how much money was there in investments?

"During that time you can also list the property for sale with Farley and that'll be all we'll need you for," Harlan continued. "You can go home and the rest of the transaction can be handled by fax and phone once the place is sold."

Why didn't that reassure her? It sounded simple—just fill out a few forms, sign some papers and let the executor handle the rest. Maybe that was the problem. It sounded *too* simple. She was eager to find out the full value of Aunt Aretha's estate, but now wasn't the time to go into that. Also, she wanted her own appraisal on the value of the property.

Sorry, Harlan, old boy, but you're not going to get rid of me that easily. I'm going to hang around for a while and see what's going on.

When they turned onto Red Robin Lane, Jodi spotted Rick's personal car parked at the curb in front of Aretha's house, the same moderately priced silver-gray foreign sports auto he'd driven to his parents' home last night, and she breathed a sigh of relief. Not that she'd thought he wouldn't show up, but she didn't want to spend too much time alone with Harlan in that spooky place.

"Well, well, it looks like the cop has arrived before a crime has even been committed," he muttered sourly, more to himself than to her, as he pulled in behind the car.

They got out and were met on the porch by Rick coming out of the house. It was the first time Jodi had seen him without his uniform, and a delightful sight he was. Great as he'd looked in it, he was even sexier in the tight jeans and T-shirt he'd donned for the dirty work they were about to do. In spite of the low temperature he wasn't wearing a jacket, and she could see the muscles in his bare arms ripple when he moved them. His broad chest tapered down to a slender waist and flat belly above powerful thighs that looked as if they'd been molded into the legs of his jeans.

With difficulty she dragged her gaze upward and it collided with his, which was as penetrating as hers. They both smiled. "Did you sleep well last night?" he asked softly, sending tiny shivers up her spine.

"Like a contented kitten," she assured him. "In fact, I overslept, but your mom wouldn't let me leave the house until I'd eaten a bowl of cereal with fruit and a slice of toast." She chuckled. "I'm warning you, I could get used to pampering like that really fast. I just may never go back home."

Rick chuckled, too, but Harlan wasn't amused. "I told you," he scolded. "There's no need for you to stay here until we get the house sold."

That brought Jodi back to earth. The man had absolutely no sense of humor. "I was only teasing," she said shortly, then focused again on Rick. "How did you get into the house, Rick? I called that locksmith you recommended and he said he'd fix the lock."

Rick looked thoughtful. "Apparently he hasn't gotten around to it yet. It's still broken. If he doesn't come while we're here I'll call and light a fire under him."

The rest of the morning was spent sorting through what could only be labeled as trash. Anything that might have been of value had been broken or smashed during the vandalism, but newspapers and magazines were stacked all over the house, making a dangerous fire hazard.

Thank God the furnace, the telephone and the electricity were still working so they had light, heat and communication with the rest of the town. Rick called the fire department and alerted them to the fire hazard. They said they'd send someone with a truck to pick up the papers and turn them in to the recycling center, then donate the money in Aretha's name to the Burn Institute sponsored by firefighters.

Jodi was delighted that something good would come from her aunt's tragic mental derangement. She suspected this cleanup was going to be expensive, and was relieved when Harlan told her it would be billed to the estate and not to her personally. Of course, either way she'd be paying for it, but not out of her salary at the preschool.

At noon they broke for hamburgers and fries at the local drive-in, and after that Rick excused himself to go back to work at the police station while Jodi and Harlan continued their depressing task. As she picked up broken pieces and put them in a plastic trash bag she realized that most of them were crystal, china and porcelain, not the cheaper objects she'd first assumed them to be. Also, several of the pictures that had been slashed were original oil and watercolors, not prints.

Later that evening Rick again came to supper at his parents' home, and she voiced her dismay. "Why would anyone destroy such lovely and expensive objects? They were obviously not looking for valuables. It's as if their only purpose was to demolish."

She turned to look at Rick. "Is there much of that kind of thing happening here in Copper Canyon?"

He shook his head. "Almost never. Oh, once in a while some of the kids will spray-paint graffiti on a fence or the side of a run-down structure, and we have a few burglaries during the course of a year, but apparently nothing has been stolen from your aunt's place. I've never seen a building trashed so badly."

"But why?" It was more of a wail than a question. "Was Aunt Aretha disliked that much? And if so, why did someone wait until after she was dead to do it? An act of revenge is only effective when the victim can be hurt by it."

"I have no idea, honey," Rick said, and the endearment sent a wave of pleasure through Jodi, even though it was a throwaway remark that he probably didn't realize he'd used.

Dorothy spoke up. "I don't see how Aretha could have

stirred up that much venom in anyone. She never went out of her yard, and seldom even ventured outside the house."

"I've talked to the neighbors," Rick said, "but that's such a sparsely populated area that there are none close enough to notice what's going on. Whoever did it was quiet about it. Nobody heard anything."

Later that evening as Rick stood to leave he asked Jodi to walk him to the car. Her heart sped up and she readily agreed. She liked his tender leave-takings!

When they walked out the door they were hit by a brisk breeze, and she realized that the temperature had dropped considerably since late afternoon. Rick was dressed in slacks and a cotton shirt topped with a cardigan sweater, which he'd worn all evening, but the pullover sweater she wore with her slacks was lightweight and short sleeved, which didn't offer much protection from the chill.

"Has Mom told you about the potluck supper and dance at the lodge hall Saturday night?" he asked as they approached his car.

This was the first she'd heard of it, but it sounded like fun. "No, she hasn't. Is Saturday a holiday or something?" Halloween was coming up, but it was still a week away.

Rick laughed. "No, nothing like that. This is a town party sponsored by the lodge on the third Saturday of every month. Everyone's welcome. All they have to do is bring a hot dish, salad or dessert to share. After supper there's dancing to live music if they can get it, otherwise it's recordings."

They'd reached the car and stopped by the passenger side. "It may not sound like much to a city girl, but it's a big event around here," he continued. "Would you consider going with me?"

He was asking her for a date! That was the important thing. It wouldn't have mattered *where* he wanted to take her, but this sounded like a blast. Also, it would give her a chance to meet more of the townspeople.

"I'd love to," she said enthusiastically just as a gust of wind blew cold air right through her thin sweater. She shivered and wrapped her arms around herself for protection.

Rick muttered an oath, then quickly stripped off his cardigan and draped it around her. "You're freezing!" he accused and enveloped her in his arms. "Why didn't you tell me? You should have put on a jacket."

Jodi's arms were pinned to her sides by both Rick's sweater and his arms, but that was fine with her. He held her close, and even without a wrap he radiated body heat and warmed her. Both physically and emotionally! She leaned into his embrace and buried her cold face in his shoulder. He rubbed his cheek in her hair, and his breath felt warm on her neck. He paused there for a moment, and his lips moved lightly against her flesh, sending ripples of pleasure down her body in all directions.

"You'll get cold without your sweater," she murmured softly as he cuddled her even closer.

"Not with you in my arms, I won't," he assured her huskily, and she could feel his heart pounding in time with her own.

She wished her arms were free to hold him, too, but she was afraid to move for fear he'd think she wanted him to release her.

She sighed and hoped that this moment would never end, but she knew it would; it had to. Even so, it was long before she was ready that he raised his head and stepped back, loosening his hold on her.

She swallowed an involuntary cry of protest, but the magic had been broken. "I'll either see you or call to make arrangements for Saturday night," he said in a tone that wasn't as impersonal as he probably wanted her to think. Or was she just hearing what she wanted to hear?

He released her completely and started around the back of the car. "Get back in the house," he ordered, "and don't worry about the sweater. I'll pick it up next time I come over. See ya. 'Night."

He was in the car and gone before she'd collected her wits about her.

On the following day, Friday, Jodi had an appointment to meet and talk with the real estate agent, Farley Finch, about putting the Coldwell property up for sale. Harlan had arranged it, and he was going to meet them for a three-way conference at Finch Realty, which, he told her, was housed on the second floor of the old two-story Churchill building on Main Street.

It seemed that Harlan wanted to be in on everything concerning her aunt's estate, and Jodi wondered if he thought she was too stupid to understand business dealings. However, she didn't argue. She had nothing to hide.

She arrived at the appointed time of ten to find Harlan already there and closeted with Mr. Finch in his office. It was a suite of two rooms, and the redheaded secretary in the reception room announced her before ushering her into the inner sanctum.

The two men stood when Jodi entered, and the one behind the desk walked over and held out his hand. "I'm Farley Finch, Ms. Hopkins," he said and shook her hand. "Please, sit down." He motioned to a chair beside Harlan at the front of the desk.

"Now then," he said as they all took their seats, "I understand you're interested in listing the Coldwell property for sale. I'm sorry about your aunt's death, and also about the vandalism at the house." He shook his head. "Must have been transients. I can't believe that anybody around here would do such a thing."

Jodi watched Finch as he spoke. She'd guess he was in his middle forties, although his hairline had receded all the way to the back of his head, leaving only a fringe of dark hair on the sides and back. He wasn't much taller than her five foot five, but was considerably overweight, with a round belly that even his double-breasted suit coat couldn't hide.

"Thank you," Jodi said, acknowledging his condolences. "I didn't know Aunt Aretha and had no contact with her or Copper Canyon, so I'm totally in the dark. I've no idea what homes sell for here. I realize the house is run down, but I noticed yesterday when I was scooping out all that trash that it seems to be sturdily built. Surely it could be fixed up and made livable."

He tapped the top of his pen on the desk. "I doubt it," he said regretfully. "The foundation needs a lot of work, and the porch and steps leading up to it are downright dangerous. Also, the electrical wiring is old and needs to be replaced, as do the water pipes. The repairs would probably cost more than the house is worth."

Jodi wasn't so sure. Granted, she knew next to nothing about construction, but it seemed to her that it would be a lot less costly to fix it up than to tear it down and build a new one. At least it was worth a try before she discounted the house altogether and sold the property for just what the land would bring. She had nothing to lose but a little extra time.

"I'm sorry, but I don't agree, Mr. Finch." She tried to keep her tone pleasant. "I'd like to get someone to clean up the grounds, replace the steps and reinforce the porch, then try selling it as a fixer-upper."

It was Harlan who reacted. "But that would take time—"

Finch shot him a disgruntled look, then smiled at Jodi. "First, call me Farley, and I'll call you Jodi if I may."

She nodded. "Of course."

"And second, how long were you planning on staying here? It would be pretty difficult to supervise repairs from halfway across the country."

"It shouldn't take more than a week to do what I have

in mind,'' she insisted. ''That is, if we can find laborers to do it. Once we get that jungle of trees and vines cut back and let the sunshine in, it won't look so creepy, and we can list it while the repairs are being done. The fact that we're doing them should be a selling point.''

''Now look here—'' Harlan broke in, but Farley once again shushed him with a look.

''With the economy what it is I'm sure you won't have trouble finding people to work,'' Farley assured her. ''I can arrange it for you if you're determined to go ahead, but I have to tell you I think you'd just be throwing good money after bad. Don't forget, that place has a reputation for being haunted. Now you and I know that's just silly superstition, but still it's a powerful impediment.''

Jodi shivered. No, she hadn't forgotten. ''I realize that, but once the area is cleared and the lawn is tended to, it won't look nearly so spooky and foreboding.''

She smiled at Farley, hoping to soften what she was about to say. ''I know you're the expert on the subject, but I want to discuss this with the McBrides before I make a decision. They've lived here all their lives and must have a pretty good idea what property is worth in Copper Canyon on today's market. I'd just like to know what they think about my suggestions.''

Harlan scowled and half rose from his chair. ''But that's—''

''That's fine,'' Farley quickly intervened, and Harlan closed his mouth and dropped back down. ''You do that. Meanwhile, I'll check out a few things, too, and we'll meet again on—'' he consulted his desk calendar ''—Monday at one o'clock?''

Jodi nodded. ''Great,'' she said and stood. ''I'll see you on Monday, then.''

She looked at Harlan. They'd spent so much time at the house the day before that it had been too late to return to the office to discuss the rest of her estate, so they'd rescheduled that for today. "And I'll see you this afternoon at two-thirty."

When Jodi arrived back at the McBride home at noon she was surprised and delighted to find Rick there. He was back in uniform and she was impressed all over again. Just looking at him made her dream impossible dreams.

"I hadn't expected you to be here for lunch," she told him as they seated themselves at the table. "But I'm glad you are. There's something I need to talk to you about."

An uncertain smile crossed his face. "Nothing bad, I hope. I wanted to talk with you, too, about the potluck tomorrow night, so I just came over and hoped Mom would invite me to stay."

"You don't need an invitation," Dorothy reproached him. "This is your home, for heaven's sake. You're always welcome."

He grinned. "I know, Ma. I was only kidding." He looked at Jodi, and the tenderness in his eyes made her heart skip a few beats. "What was it you wanted to talk to me about? Can we discuss it here, or would you rather wait?"

She realized he'd misunderstood and thought she wanted to speak to him privately. "Well, actually, I wanted to talk to both you *and* your parents. I need some information and advice."

"We'll be glad to help any way we can," Shawn said. "What seems to be the problem?"

Jodi told them about her conversation with Farley and Harlan, and when she'd finished it was Shawn who spoke first. "I'd suggest that you get an independent appraiser in to go over the house and property and give you his opinion of its worth. It will cost you, but I think it would be money well spent."

"I agree," Rick said. "Those old houses were built to last practically forever, and they also have historical value.

In the cities now, the historical societies are fighting to save the antique homes from being torn down."

"Our house is nearly the same age as Aretha's," Dorothy said, "and it's solid as a rock. I admit the Coldwell place hasn't been kept up the way it should have been, but I'm betting the construction is still solid. It just needs a little shoring up and a lot of soap and water and paint."

"I can check around and find you an appraiser if you'd like," Rick assured her. "I have contacts in Boise. I'll look up the appropriate state agency and ask for some referrals."

Her knight in shining armor to the rescue again, Jodi thought as she spoke around the lump in her throat. "Oh, would you, Rick? I'm sorry to put you to so much trouble, but..."

He put his hand over hers where it lay on the table. "It's no trouble," he assured her softly. "In fact, I suspect I'd do almost anything for you—"

He stopped abruptly and withdrew his hand, probably because he remembered suddenly that they weren't alone.

After a slight pause during which nobody broke the silence, he spoke again. "Okay, now that that's settled, how about if I pick you up tomorrow night at six? Don't worry about food to take. I'm bringing my famous chili."

Shawn chuckled. "He always brings his famous chili. That's why it's famous."

Rick laughed, too. "You bet. All I have to do is assemble all the ingredients in the Crock-Pot in the morning and turn it to Low. By late afternoon it's all ready to eat."

It occurred to Jodi that he was almost too good to be true. Not only handsome, sexy, gentle and successful, but he could also cook! What woman could ask for more? If only she could take him home with her.

Several hours later she left Harlan Lowery's office in a shock-induced daze. She'd finally learned the full extent of her inheritance, and her mind was still trying to absorb it.

Aunt Aretha had left her enough money invested in blue-chip stocks, bonds and certificates of deposit that she could live as well as she did now on the interest alone without ever working again!

Chapter Four

Saturday was a beautiful day, bright with sunshine and not even a breeze to chill the warmth of it. Jodi didn't think she'd ever been quite so happy. Why shouldn't she be? She was financially secure for the rest of her life.

Not that she intended to quit work. She loved working with the children too much to do that, but with her salary, as well as the monthly interest checks, she could live very comfortably. It was like a dream come true and totally unexpected.

If Aunt Aretha had had that much money, why had she lived in such squalor? Oh, Jodi had studied psychology and sociology in college, and knew about the mental aberrations that made some people do strange things, but why had it happened to her aunt? She apparently hadn't been a very likable person, since she'd long been estranged from her family, but unlikable didn't necessarily mean unbalanced. It was a question that would probably never be answered, but Jodi silently vowed to use some of the money to further the study of such derangements and a possible cure.

She hadn't told Rick or the McBrides the extent of her

inheritance, and had warned Harlan not to mention it to anybody. He'd been insulted by her request and told her angrily that he never discussed bank business except with those whom it concerned. She believed him, but was still glad she'd left no doubt about her wishes. She didn't intend to discuss her personal finances with anyone, except, of course, the Internal Revenue Service. That thought was a daunting one!

Today, however, her full attention was given over to the supper and dance tonight, and she asked Dorothy what she should wear. All she had with her were jeans, slacks, a few tops and a couple of dresses.

"It's strictly casual," Dorothy told her. "Most of the men wear Western-style pants, shirts and boots, and a lot of the women wear full skirts and low-heeled shoes for easy dancing. Sort of like square-dance costumes. In fact, we used to have a square-dance group in town. It was real popular, but then the caller moved away and we never found anyone to replace him."

Her gaze roamed over Jodi. "You look to be about the same size as my daughter," she said thoughtfully. "Jessica left her square-dance dresses here when she and her husband moved to Boise. I'm sure they'd fit you. Why don't you try one on?"

Jodi was delighted with the suggestion and even more so when all three dresses did indeed fit. She chose the purple crinkly cotton one with a three-tiered skirt. There was a bouffant net petticoat to wear with it, but she decided against it. It was too bulky since they wouldn't be square dancing.

"You look lovely," Dorothy assured her as she twirled for inspection. "You'll be the belle of the ball, and that's for sure."

Jodi doubted that, but hoped she'd be a hit with Rick.

Shawn and Dorothy also planned to attend, and when they all four assembled in the living room that evening before leaving, Shawn and Rick were wearing the type of Western outfits Dorothy had described earlier, and Rick's mom looked especially pretty in dark turquoise slacks and a matching loose pullover tunic. With it she wore a turquoise Native American style necklace and earrings.

"Dorothy, if I didn't know better I'd think you were Rick's older sister instead of his mother," Jodi said, and meant it. "You look positively smashing."

Dorothy blushed but her eyes sparkled with excitement.

"She's as beautiful today as she was the day I met her," Shawn said, and the admiration in his tone was genuine.

Her blush deepened as she said thank-you to them both, then smiled tenderly at her husband as the men helped the women into their coats. The two couples left for the lodge hall in separate cars.

Rick eyed Jodi in the seat beside him. "I really like your dress." His voice was husky. "That color brings out a hint of violet in those beautiful blue eyes of yours."

A warm, happy feeling stole over her. "It's your sister's dress." Her tone was husky, too. "Your mom loaned it to me."

He reached over and took her hand. "Well, Jessica always did have a good sense of design. I don't remember her wearing it, but it looks great on you."

"Thank you." She squeezed his hand and he squeezed back, then changed the subject.

"I made arrangements for an appraiser to come from Lewiston on Tuesday of next week to look over your property. Sorry I wasn't able to get hold of you to confirm it, but I can reschedule if that's not convenient."

She was learning that when Rick McBride said he'd do something he did it, and quickly.

"That's fine," she said. "Thank you, Rick. I can't tell you how much I appreciate your doing this. I hate to be such a bother."

He brought her hand up to his mouth and kissed her

knuckles. "You could never be a bother," he murmured against the back of her hand before he released it and put both of his on the steering wheel to guide the car over to the curb and park.

The lodge hall was a rectangular building that consisted of one large room plus a small kitchen and rest-room facilities at one end. There was a stage at the opposite end where a large stereo system had been set up, which no doubt meant that the music tonight would be recorded instead of live. Rows of fold up tables and chairs lined the floor, and buffet tables along the back wall already held a tempting array of food.

They spotted Rick's parents in a group of people over by the stage and waved as they made their way across the room to deposit Rick's Crock-Pot full of chili with the rest of the hot dishes. Their progress was hampered by people greeting Rick. Then he'd introduce Jodi and explain who she was, which started up another turn of the conversation so that most of the folks were already seated by the time they got around to finding a place at the tables.

Rick introduced the good-looking couple sitting beside them as Jim and Coralie Buckley. "Jim's a farmer," he told Jodi, "and also chairman of the county board of supervisors."

After the usual condolences over her aunt's death Jodi and Coralie, who were sitting side by side, continued talking. Coralie was obviously pregnant, and Jodi asked when the baby was due.

"Two more months," Coralie said happily, "and we already know it's a boy."

Jodi felt a stab of envy. Someday, God willing, she'd be saying things like that. "That's great," she said enthusiastically. "Is it your first child?"

"Not really—Jim has two teenage daughters who live with us, but I consider them mine, too. This is our first son, though."

What a nice person, Jodi thought. It was obvious from the way they looked at each other that she and her husband were very much in love. Jodi wished she was going to be in this hospitable little town long enough to get to know them better. She was almost certain she and Coralie had a lot in common and could become close friends.

The more she thought of it, the more she realized that when she left Copper Canyon she'd be leaving a lot of good people, and things, behind. Although it hadn't occurred to her before, now that she had an independent income she could live almost anywhere she wanted to without worrying about whether or not she'd find work quickly. Still, Cincinnati was her home. She knew it well and felt comfortable with her life there. If only Rick—

She quickly banished that line of thinking and concentrated on all the delicious-looking food heaped on her plate. No sense in wishing for the moon. Rick would never leave Copper Canyon. Nor should he. He'd done that once when he'd joined the Detroit police department, but it hadn't worked out. His family, his roots and his heart were here.

An hour or so later, when everyone had finished eating, the tables and chairs were folded up and put in a storage space under the stage, and the disc jockey took his place at the stereo console.

Much to Jodi's delight the first piece was a rousing polka, and her toes started tapping involuntarily to the rhythm. Rick took her hand and led her to the dance floor, then put one hand at her waist and held the other one as they pranced and whirled around the room.

Jodi loved it. It had been years since she'd danced a polka. The music in Cincinnati tended more toward rock and roll, or rhythm and blues, but the lively polka allowed her to shed all her inhibitions and soar.

When the melody stopped it took her a moment to come back down to earth, but when she did, Rick was holding her in his arms while waiting for the next song to begin.

He'd held her like this the night before while trying to keep her sheltered from the cold breeze, but this was different. Not as private, but more intimate somehow. He wasn't trying to keep her warm, he was simply doing it because he wanted to.

They were both breathing heavily from the brisk pace of the dance, and their hearts pounded against each other's chests. Her soft breasts pushed against his hard pectorals, and he pressed her abdomen into his flat belly as his fingers unobtrusively caressed her lower back.

Before either of them could speak the music started up again. This time it was a country western ballad, slow and throbbing with emotion. Rick left both arms around her waist, and she put hers around his neck as they moved slowly into the rhythm. They were bonded together from their cheeks to their knees, and she could feel the muscles of his thighs and his stomach pull and loosen as they moved in time with the sensuous beat.

Very soon she felt another of his muscles, a far more intimate one, that had hardened and made itself known to both of them. Jodi was both embarrassed and excited. This proved that he wasn't indifferent to her after all, and she sure wasn't dispassionate toward him.

With a soft groan he pressed her even closer and she molded herself to him willingly. "Now you know what you do to me," he murmured raggedly into her ear.

She shivered and said the only thing that came to mind. "Yes. I...I'm sorry."

He leaned his head back slightly and looked at her. His brown eyes were nearly black with passion. "Are you really?"

She couldn't lie to him, didn't even want to. "Only if you are," she admitted.

He put his cheek back against her hair. "You know there can never be anything lasting between us, don't you?"

That was not what she wanted to hear him say, but she

had to admit it was true. "That's what I've been telling myself."

"And do you believe it?"

She moved her head so that she could put her cheek against his. His face was freshly shaved and smelled clean and male. "I'm not sure. My mind tells me it's true, but then you come around and my good sense gets lost in the clamor of other, more powerful, emotions."

He hugged her, hard, then straightened up. "Dammit, Jodi, you're driving me crazy. Let's get out of here."

He danced her over to the door, then took her hand and they strode out of the lodge hall.

It was chilly outside, and once again she was without her coat, which she'd left inside. Rick took off his jacket and helped her put it on.

"Walk with me," he said, then turned and headed north on the sidewalk. "I can't go back in there like this."

Jodi, walking briskly beside him, couldn't stifle a giggle, and he turned his head to look at her. "You think it's funny, don't you?" He didn't sound upset, just frustrated.

She sobered. "No, Rick, not funny, just, well, flattering. I'm glad I affect you that way."

He stopped walking and turned toward her. They were under a streetlamp so they could see each other clearly.

For a moment she was afraid she'd angered him, but then he chuckled and put his hands on her upper arms. "You little wench." His tone was soft and indulgent. "You've been giving me a bad time ever since I first set eyes on you. It's not something I welcome, so why are you so happy about it?"

She looked down, feeling a little ashamed. She didn't want him to suffer because of her, but the fact that he did aroused her intensely. She couldn't help feeling glad to know that she did the same thing to him.

"Because I'm strongly attracted to you," she confessed. "I know nothing can come of it. We live hundreds of miles from each other, and have different interests and goals, but I can't help how I feel.''

She took a deep breath and decided to level even further with him. ''Rick, if I were willing to give up my life in Cincinnati and move to Copper Canyon, would it make a difference to you?''

A look of surprise twisted his face and she hurried on. ''Oh, I'm not asking for a commitment or anything. I realize we'd have to get to know each other a lot better than we do now, take our time and so forth, but if the obstacle of distance was removed, is there a chance that you might want me? For more than just a vacation fling, I mean.''

The look of surprise was replaced by one of anguish, and his hands tightened on her arms. ''Dammit, Jodi, haven't you been listening to anything I've been saying? I want you now. I'd sell my soul to spend the night making love with you and let nature take its course, but I'm not going to. Not now or ever.''

She felt as if she'd had the breath knocked out of her. A swooshing ''Oh'' was all she could manage.

Her confusion and embarrassment must have shown on her face because he wrapped his arms around her and held her tight. ''I'm sorry, sweetheart,'' he said huskily. ''I'm really botching this, aren't I? I didn't mean that as a rejection but as a last-ditch effort to ward off a lot of pain for both of us.''

He gripped her tightly, then released her. ''It's too cold to linger out here. Let's get in the car and turn on the heater. We can drive around while we talk.''

Rick's small sports car warmed up quickly as he slowly cruised the streets of the quiet little town and tried to make order out of the chaos of his thoughts. He didn't want to hurt her, but he had to make her understand what he wanted to say. Or rather, what he *needed* to say.

She sat quietly beside him, looking sad and perplexed, and he silently cursed his traitorous body. He'd been telling himself he could keep his male urges hidden and under control, but he hadn't taken into account the fact that part of the time tonight they'd be dancing close together to slow and romantic music. Once he had her in his arms their bodies melded together so amorously that it was impossible to control or hide his arousal.

Now he knew he was playing with fire, and it was time to put a stop to it.

He took a deep breath and plunged ahead before he could chicken out. His problem wasn't one that could be kept secret from a lover for long, and once it was known she'd never forgive him for deceiving her. "Jodi, there's another, far stronger, reason than just distance why we can never have a romantic relationship. I've known it all along and I should never have allowed even a friendship between us, but I gotta tell you, sweetheart, you're a hard woman to ignore."

She finally looked up, and he tried for a smile but suspected he wasn't too successful.

"I—I'm sorry if I've been a nuisance," she stammered. "I didn't mean to..."

Rick gripped the steering wheel in order to keep from taking her hand, or putting his hand on her thigh, but he knew that if he touched her he'd be lost.

"No, that's not what I mean," he hastened to assure her. "If you hadn't asked me for help I'd have volunteered it. Right from that first day I couldn't stay away from you. Your sunny smile, the breathless way you speak and the warmth of your touch were irresistible."

"Then I don't understand," she said plaintively. "If you're attracted to me—"

"I'm more than just attracted," he interrupted. "I'm obsessed, but I told myself that as long as I kept it light—no kissing, no intimate touching—it wouldn't do any harm to continue to see you."

He shook his head in self-derision. "After what happened tonight I know that's no longer possible. I'm in much deeper than I thought. Just being with you is no longer enough, and a short-term sexual relationship would bring more anguish than pleasure when it ended."

She lowered her head again. "But why would it have to end? I mean if we...if we learned to love each other—"

He sighed. She still didn't understand. "You don't *learn* to love. Either it happens or it doesn't, and marriage for us is out of the question."

Her head jerked up then, and though it was too dark to see her expression, her tone of voice told him what she was feeling. "Oh, for heaven's sake, Rick, stop beating around the bush and get to the point. What is it that makes it so impossible?"

A look of dawning comprehension flitted across her face. "My God, you're not married, are you?"

Her accusation was like a punch in the gut. How could she even think such a thing of him? On the other hand, from the way he was pussyfooting around, that would seem to be a logical conclusion. "No, Jodi! I'm hurt that you even had to ask."

She looked relieved, and he realized that he'd tried her patience to the breaking point. "All right, I'm sorry I'm taking so long about this. You've mentioned several times that you want babies, lots of them."

"Yes, I do." Her voice had softened as it always did when she spoke of children. "But what has that got to do with—"

"I don't want kids, Jodi." His tone was rougher than he'd intended. "When I get married it will be to a woman who is equally uninterested in having a family."

She sat as if stunned before she finally spoke. "Don't want children? But why? Doesn't everyone want to raise a family?"

He shook his head. "No, not everybody. Some folks just plain don't like kids, and more and more women nowadays are intent on getting ahead in a career and don't want to jeopardize it by taking time off to have and raise babies. There's nothing wrong with that, and that's the kind of woman I want for a wife. The world is fast becoming overpopulated, anyway.''

Rick cringed as he imagined the scorn she must feel for him. She was the earth-mother type and would never understand why a man wouldn't want to father children. Still, he'd known this would happen, and he had to carry it out to the end. There was no other way.

''Are you one of those people who doesn't like kids?'' she asked.

She sounded so disbelieving and he wanted her approval so desperately that he couldn't lie, but neither could he tell her the whole truth.

''Sure I like them, other people's, but I'm not prepared to bring them into a world as violent and chaotic as ours.''

''But our children are our hope for a better world,'' she said reasonably. ''Without them we have no future.''

Rick was conscious of a dull throbbing pain in his head, and a queasiness in his stomach. This discussion was going on too long and it was too painful for both of them to drag it out any longer. It was time to end it.

''There are many people like you who will bear and raise our future generation,'' he responded. ''I feel strongly that men or women who don't want children shouldn't have them. They seldom make good parents.

''Anyway, now you know why we can never be anything but the most casual friends. I won't change my mind, and I would never ask you to change yours. You'd soon come to hate me if I did.''

She didn't deny it; in fact, she didn't speak at all, and when he looked around him he realized that after driving aimlessly for more than an hour the car, like the carriage horses of old, had managed to find its way home to the neighborhood where his parents lived. It was just as well; he couldn't take much more of this.

A few minutes later he pulled up in front of the family home and stopped. "It's getting late," he explained when she looked at him questioningly. "The dancing only lasts until eleven, so there's not much point in going back. Do you mind? I'm afraid my self-control would never survive another encounter like that last one on the dance floor."

She straightened up and pushed the handle to open the door. "No, I don't mind," she said crisply, "and please don't come up to the house with me."

She stepped out of the car, and he scrambled out on his side and hurried around to meet her on the sidewalk. "I have to unlock the door for you," he reminded her. "You didn't bring a purse, and I don't think Mom and Dad are home yet."

Together they walked up the walkway to the house and Rick unlocked the door and pushed it open. The living room was well lit. His parents always left lights on when they weren't home in the evenings.

He stepped inside with her. "I'll pick up your coat and my Crock-Pot at the lodge hall first thing in the morning. They'll be okay there overnight."

He turned to face her, and that was a mistake. She looked so forlorn and rejected in spite of all his assurances that such wasn't the case. His resolve shattered. He reached out to stroke his hands through her hair and cup her head on either side.

"I—I guess this is goodbye, more or less," he stammered around the knot in his throat. "We'll see each other from time to time while you're here, of course, but I won't be asking you out again. You do understand why, don't you?"

Their glances met and clung. "Yes, I think so," she said in little more than a whisper. "Thanks for all your help and, well, it's been nice knowing you."

With just a slight downward movement his forehead touched hers. "If there was anything I could do to make things different, I would," he murmured, just a breath away from her parted lips. If either of them puckered it would be a kiss, and he couldn't let that happen.

With every bit of willpower he could muster, he dropped his hands and backed away from her, then turned and walked out of the house.

Jodi shut the door and leaned against it. She felt drained, as if she'd had all the energy squeezed out of her.

What had happened? She and Rick had been having such a good time, and then, all of a sudden, all the gaiety had turned to despair. It had occurred so quickly that she still wasn't able to assimilate his reasoning.

He'd said he didn't want children, but was that really true? She thought everyone wanted a family. He claimed he had strong feelings for her, but he wasn't going to get involved with her because he didn't want to raise kids.

Jodi found that unfathomable. Rick wasn't that rigid. To the contrary, he was one of the most generous and giving men she'd ever met. He was so empathetic. So sensitive to other people's feelings. Even tonight he'd struggled to tell her about his decision without hurting or humiliating her. He hadn't been successful; she was both hurt and humiliated, but at least he'd tried.

Pushing herself away from the door she started up the stairs. It was only then that she realized she was still wearing his jacket, and she took it off and carried it up with her. She didn't want to be around when Dorothy and Shawn came home. They'd be curious as to why she and Rick had left the dance before it was over and why he'd brought her home so early, but how could she explain it to them when she didn't understand it herself?

Apparently she'd failed him in some way and he was trying to break off with her as painlessly as possible. She couldn't believe that he just didn't want to raise a family.

It didn't fit with his personality. Oh, maybe he didn't want a big family like she did, but neither was he the type who actively disliked children.

At the top of the stairs she hurried down the hall to the bathroom to wash her face and brush her teeth and get back to her room and into bed before his parents came in. She'd have to face them at breakfast, but she just couldn't do it any sooner.

After a restless night Jodi finally fell asleep shortly after she heard the beautiful old antique grandfather clock in the living room strike three o'clock. Then she didn't wake up in the morning until just in time to dress and hurry downstairs to say goodbye to Shawn and Dorothy as they left for church.

She felt wretched as she sat alone at the table with a cup of strong black coffee and struggled with her agonizing thoughts. One thing was certain. She couldn't stay here with Rick's folks any longer; it would be too awkward. He'd made it plain that he didn't want anything more to do with her, so he wouldn't want her living with his parents any longer, either.

She'd already decided that she'd pack her things and make some excuse for moving to the motel on the highway. Glancing around the spotless kitchen she blinked back tears. She'd been made welcome here and felt so at home. The McBrides were such friendly and hospitable people. How was she ever going to leave without offending them?

On the other hand she couldn't stay here, because then Rick wouldn't feel free to breeze in and out of his parents' home the way he always did.

Jodi could take a hint. She'd been confused last night, but by morning she had it figured out. Rick had come to realize that his attraction to her had been a passing fancy and he didn't want to get serious, but neither did he have the heart to just tell her that. So he'd made up the story about wanting her but not wanting children, and hoped it would soften the inevitable blow to her pride.

She grimaced. Well, it didn't. Apparently he wasn't aware that he was a lousy liar. On the other hand this was a new experience. She'd never been dumped before so it was probably bound to happen sometime.

By the time she finished her third cup of coffee it tasted bitter, and she was disgusted with her self-pitying retrospection. It was time to get her act together and pack up.

She was upstairs in her room going through the dresser drawers to make sure she hadn't forgotten anything when she heard the front door open downstairs and a voice called, "Hi. Anybody home?"

It was Rick! But what was he doing here? He'd made it plain last night that he didn't want to see her again, so he could have at least given her time to move out of the house before coming over. Her first inclination was to not answer and hope he'd leave, but she quickly discarded it. She'd feel pretty silly if he came upstairs and found her.

Dammit, she wasn't going to run and hide like a timid mouse every time he came into view. She'd be in town for a while yet, and she wasn't going to let him know how close she'd come to falling in love with him.

She walked to the top of the stairs and looked down. He was standing in the spacious entry way with something folded over his arm. "Rick," she called, and he looked up and saw her. "Your parents aren't home from church yet. They said something about staying after the service for a committee meeting. Can I give them a message?"

He watched her as she walked self-consciously down the stairs. She wished he wouldn't do that. It was hard enough to keep her expression pleasant but disinterested without being scrutinized so closely. He looked so...so bleak, and it was all she could do to keep from throwing herself in his arms when she got close enough to him.

"I brought your coat," he said and took the garment off his arm and handed it to her.

Well, so much for her wild imagination. He only wanted to return her coat.

"Thank you," she said as she took it from him. "I'm glad you arrived with it before I left. Yours is upstairs in my room."

He frowned. "Left?"

"Yes," she said and was relieved that her voice didn't quiver. "I was just packing."

The frown turned to a scowl. "What do you mean, packing? I thought your aunt's estate hadn't been settled yet."

She hung her coat in the closet under the stairs. "It hasn't. I'm just moving to the motel."

"No!" It was a command, not a request, and she stiffened with resentment. He wasn't going to toss her aside and then order her around!

Before she could voice her displeasure he backed down. "I'm sorry, Jodi, I didn't mean that the way it sounded, but if you're leaving here because of something I said last night, then please don't. I'd like for you to stay with Mom and Dad. They enjoy having you here, and...and so do I."

Now she was more confused than ever. "I thought you didn't want anything more to do with me."

For the first time she noticed how tired he looked. His face was more gray than rosy, and there were dark circles under his eyes. She knew that under her carefully applied makeup she didn't look much better. He must not have slept much, either.

When he spoke again even his voice sounded weary. "Jodi, I don't know how you could have misconstrued what I was telling you last night to mean that, but you've got it all wrong. I want you to stay here. It's so much more comfortable than any motel you'll find around Copper Canyon, and the folks have plenty of room. If you're worried about running into me too often, don't. I don't usually spend a lot of time here."

He put his hand on the doorknob. "I'm on duty today and I have to get back to the station, but please promise me you won't move out until you've had more time to think it over."

Chapter Five

Jodi's pride told her to refuse Rick's request, but her common sense warned her she'd be a fool to give up a tastefully decorated, warm, homey room and board in the McBride home to hole up in a skimpy, cheap and lonely motel room. She hadn't asked to stay here, the McBrides had invited her, and pride could be a desolate bedfellow.

"Well, if you're sure it won't be an inconvenience I'll stay," she said haltingly. "But only for a few more days. Harlan Lowery is probably right—I don't need to be here until the house is sold."

"Don't let him or anyone else rush you, Jodi," Rick said seriously. "Take your time, and don't go back to Ohio until it feels right to you. It might not be a bad idea to consult a lawyer. Someone who doesn't have a stake in the outcome the way both Harlan and Farley have."

That sounded like wise advice to Jodi, and she relaxed and managed a small smile. "I'll think about it," she promised, "but I'm not going to do anything until your appraiser tells me what the property is worth."

After Rick took his jacket and left a few minutes later

she called Farley Finch's office. Since it was Sunday there was nobody there, but she left a message on his answering machine canceling her Monday appointment. She told him she was having an independent appraisal of her property and she'd get in touch with him when she got the results of that.

It was Thursday before she received those results in the mail, along with a bill, from the firm Rick had contacted in Lewiston. Although she was a little disappointed that the property wasn't evaluated for as much as she'd hoped, it was still considerably more than either Harlan or Farley had indicated.

Her first inclination was to call Rick and read the letter to him, but on second thought she decided against it. She hadn't seen or heard from him since their encounter on Sunday, and she didn't want him to think she was coming on to him again.

Instead, she read it to his mother, and Dorothy was overjoyed. "Oh, Jodi, that's great!" she exclaimed. "It seemed to Shawn and me that the agent here was too low on his estimate. I'm so glad you brought in an outsider. Have you told Rick yet?"

Jodi hesitated. So far his parents hadn't commented on the fact that Rick hadn't been around recently, but she knew they wondered about it.

"No, I...I haven't seen or talked to him lately, but I don't mind if you discuss it with him. I'm truly grateful to him for finding an independent appraiser for me."

"Then why don't you tell him yourself, dear?" Dorothy murmured. There was no censure or curiosity in her tone, but Jodi realized how ungrateful her own words had sounded.

"Yes. Of course. I will." In her confusion she sort of spit out the words in short, staccato sentences that sounded equally churlish.

"That is... I mean..." She could feel the hot blush that reddened her face.

Dorothy turned from the meat loaf she was mixing for dinner and looked at her. "Jodi, has my son done something to offend you? Has he been...ungentlemanly?"

The idea of Rick being "ungentlemanly" was so ludicrous that Jodi almost laughed but caught herself in time. What Dorothy was implying was no laughing matter, certainly not to his mother, and even the fact that she could feel compelled to ask must have pained her greatly.

"Oh, Dorothy, no!" Jodi said emphatically. "Rick is good and kind and would never be anything but a gentleman. It's just that we don't have much in common, so we decided not to...to date anymore."

"You quarreled." It wasn't a question but a statement.

Jodi shook her head vigorously. "No, truly we didn't, but I...I offered to move into a motel. Rick wouldn't hear of it. He said you liked having me here." She looked away from Dorothy's penetrating glance. "I hope that's true. I wouldn't dream of imposing on you and Shawn—"

"I told you before, you're not imposing, and I have no intention of prying into your relationship with my son. You're both adults and capable of handling your own problems. I just want you both to know that you can come to me anytime you feel a need to talk and I'll listen."

Jodi felt tears gathering in her eyes and swallowed. "I appreciate that, and if the need ever arises, I will."

A tear fell from one eye and she wiped it away with the back of her hand. "Sorry," she said timidly. "I guess I miss my own mother more than I realized. She and my stepfather live in Atlanta now so I don't see them very often."

Dorothy put the meat mixture into a loaf pan and patted it into shape. "That's too bad," she said sympathetically. "I'm so very fortunate to have my children and grandchildren fairly close, but we've always got room for one more and I'd be happy to be a substitute mother for you when you need one."

A few minutes after that Jodi dialed the police station and asked to speak to Rick. The dispatcher asked for her name and she told her, "Jodi."

He came on the line immediately. "Hello, sweethea—uh, Jodi," he stammered. "Is everything all right?" He sounded concerned.

"Everything's fine," she said with a forced gaiety. She told him about the letter. "Your mother suggested I call and read it to you," she concluded.

"Did you have to be prompted by Mom to do that?" he asked, then apparently thought better of it. "Never mind, what does it say? Good news, I hope?"

She read the letter aloud, and when she'd finished he chuckled. "I was afraid Harlan and Farley were trying to put one over on you. Are you going to fix it up or sell it 'as is'?"

"I'll get someone to do the maintenance work that needs to be done and list it as a fixer-upper. Even though the neighborhood isn't very desirable, I'd like to save the house. I think I can get a fair price without spending too much on repairs."

"Will you still list it with Finch Realty?"

"Yes, but now I know what it's worth, so I'm the one in charge. I'll call this afternoon and make an appointment to get together with Farley as soon as possible."

"And then what?" He sounded reluctant, as though the question had been dragged out of him.

She knew what he was asking. "Then I'll go back to Cincinnati. I don't want to be away any longer than I have to. Good substitute preschool teachers are difficult to find."

"I see," he said. "You will keep me posted, won't you?"

She assured him she would, and after an awkward good-bye they hung up.

She immediately dialed Finch Realty, asked for an appointment and was scheduled for three o'clock that afternoon.

Jodi arrived at Finch Realty a few minutes early, but was ushered right in to Farley's office.

"Jodi, good to see you," he said as he rose and reached across the desk to shake hands with her. "I understand you've heard from your appraiser. Sit down and tell me all about it."

"Yes, I have," she said as they both took their seats. She removed the letter from her purse and handed it to him to read.

He examined it carefully then handed it back to her. "Hartford and Durante is a prestigious old firm," he said carefully, "but I'm afraid they're a little out of touch with real estate values in the rural areas. I'm sure this would be right on the button in Lewiston, but I don't think you'll ever get that price here."

Jodi wasn't surprised that he would argue about the other firm's appraisal, but it did chip away at her confidence. What if he was right? She could waste a lot of time trying to sell at inflated prices, and meanwhile the property would stand empty and be a target for more vandalism.

He wasn't as abrasive as Harlan and didn't antagonize her as badly. Also, he was the town's only real estate agent and had been in the business for a lot of years. She had every reason to trust him, but still...

Taking a deep breath she decided to go with her gut feeling. It seldom steered her wrong. "You may be right, but since I went to the expense and trouble of getting another opinion, I think I'll go ahead and fix it up a little and list it at their price. I can always come down later if necessary."

Farley folded his hands on the desk and frowned. "I wouldn't recommend that, Jodi. You'd just be wasting both time and money.'' He brightened. ''I think I have a better idea. My realty will buy the property from you at the price I originally quoted. That way you can tie up the loose ends of your aunt's estate and go back to Cincinnati, and I can take my time trying to sell the place and not take a loss.''

Jodi doubted that Farley Finch ever took a loss on anything, and the price he offered was much too low. Although she was anxious to get home, she wasn't going to give this place away.

Now she was getting irritated. What was he up to, anyway? It was her house; she could do whatever she wanted with it. ''Are you saying you don't want to handle the listing on my terms? If so, I understand there's a real estate firm in Gainsville that—''

That got an immediate reaction as his bald head turned red. ''Oh, no! No, my dear, that's not what I'm saying at all.'' He didn't jump to his feet, but she got the impression that he had to force himself not to. ''Of course we'll list the property. I just couldn't let you spend the extra time and money without warning you that it would probably be to no avail.''

Sure he couldn't. He also wasn't going to let the competition come in and beat him out of a commission.

Shawn had told her about the firm in the little town of Gainsville, which was less than fifteen miles away and was actively competing with Finch Realty for business in Copper Canyon. She'd suspected that mentioning it would get a rise out of Farley, and she'd been so right!

She smiled sweetly. ''I understand, and thank you for being so thoughtful, but I prefer to try it my way first. If you'll have a contract drawn up I'll have my lawyer look it over and—''

''Your lawyer!'' Again his bald spot turned color.

''Why, yes, do you have some objection?'' Her voice was cool and calm but with a note of warning.

"Of...of course not," he said quickly. "You can pick up the document any time after lunch tomorrow."

The following day Jodi did just that, then took the agreement to a lawyer, Victor Stuart, whom Shawn recommended. "He's a bright young fellow who was born and raised here," Shawn had said. "Married a girl he met in college and brought her back home with him. She owns a pricey dress shop downtown called Yvonne's Boutique, and he's goin' great guns with his law practice."

Victor Stuart was indeed young—early thirties—bright and handsome with brown hair and blue eyes. He wore a well-cut navy blue business suit, and stood when his secretary ushered Jodi into his office. "Good afternoon, Ms. Hopkins." His smile was wide and genuine. "I'm Victor. Please, sit down. Shawn says you have a contract you want me to look over?"

"Good afternoon, Victor," she said and sat down across the desk from him. "I'm Jodi, and yes, I do need some advice on an agreement that Farley Finch has drawn up for me to sign."

She told him about her inheritance and explained her problems with both Harlan and Farley. "Maybe I'm being overly cautious," she concluded, "but I don't know anything about real estate or investing money and—"

"You're certainly not being overly cautious," he interrupted. "I just wish all my clients would be as careful as you are before they leap into business arrangements they know nothing about. It would save them and me a lot of grief. If you can leave this contract with me, I'll look it over during the weekend and get back to you on Monday. Okay?"

At supper that evening Jodi told Shawn and Dorothy about her day, and Shawn made a surprising offer. "If you'd like I'll go over to the house with you tomorrow morning to check on what has to be done to make it salable. We can probably do part of the work ourselves."

"Oh, but I couldn't ask you to do that," she protested.

He smiled. "You didn't ask me, I offered," he reminded her. "I've been doing all the gardening and most of the maintenance around this house ever since Dotty and I moved in shortly before our first child was born almost thirty-six years ago. I think that together you and I can handle at least part of the work over there. That is, if you want to," he hastened to add.

"I'd love to," she said on a tide of rising excitement.

"I'll come, too—" Dorothy offered.

She was interrupted by a stern, "No," from Shawn.

"You're not going to heft boards and climb trees," he insisted, then turned to Jodi. "She had heart surgery three years ago," he explained.

"I'm sorry," Jodi said. "I didn't know. Are you all right?"

"I'm fine," Dorothy said firmly. "Far better than I was before the surgery, but himself here keeps trying to make an invalid of me."

"Damn right," Shawn growled and put his hand over hers on the table. Jodi saw the shadow of fear in his eyes. "I'm not going to lose you. I came too close to that three years ago. I'd wrap you in cotton batting and keep you at home if I could get away with it."

Dorothy's expression softened, and she turned her hand over and squeezed his. "You're not going to lose me, love," she murmured tenderly and smiled. "I'm not going until you're ready to go with me. However, if it means so much to you, I'll stay home tomorrow and fix meals. You'll both be ravenous, and I'm better with a cookbook than a lawn mower or a hammer, anyway."

The next day, Saturday, Jodi was up early and eager to get started. She pulled on her oldest jeans and sweatshirt and went downstairs to put the coffee on. By the time it had finished perking Dorothy appeared and insisted on fixing bacon, eggs and biscuits for breakfast. Jodi protested, but Dorothy was one of those women who felt she wasn't feeding her family right if she didn't cook them three big meals a day plus intermittent snacks.

Shawn and Jodi finally pulled away from the house in Shawn's Oldsmobile at eight-thirty, weighed down with a trunk full of tools and other building supplies, but she noticed one omission.

"We don't have any yard equipment such as a lawn mower or a pruning saw," she commented.

"No, I don't have room for the bigger implements in the car," Shawn said. "Rick is bringing those in his truck."

Jodi's body tingled and her mind went blank. "Rick?"

No, there must be some mistake! No one had mentioned him.

"Yes," Shawn said. "Didn't I tell you? He offered to help so I asked him to bring the bigger stuff in his pickup."

"But how..." She closed her mouth and bit off the question. If she acted surprised or upset Shawn would wonder why, and they'd be back to the "did you or didn't you quarrel?" conversation that she'd had earlier with Dorothy. She'd just wait and find out from Rick how he got involved.

As they drove down Red Robin Lane Jodi saw a rather beat up blue pickup parked in front of the house. He must already be here! Shawn parked behind the truck just as Rick came around the side of the building.

Shawn opened his door and got out. "Hi," he called. "Is everything okay?"

"It seems to be," Rick called back as he headed toward them. "The door's locked and there's no sign that anyone's been snooping around."

Jodi was still gathering her wits about her as she forced herself to get out of the car and face Rick. Did he think she had anything to do with his being asked to help?

Their gazes met and held as he walked up to her. "Hello, Jodi," he said softly.

It was bad enough that he was so good-looking, but that sexy baritone voice of his sent heat straight to her core. She cleared her throat and hoped her own voice wouldn't betray her. "Rick, I didn't know you'd be here until just a few minutes ago," she told him apologetically. "I hope you don't think that I—"

"That you wanted me here," he finished for her. "I'd hoped that you did, but I can see that you didn't."

He actually sounded disappointed.

"I called Dad last night about something else, and he told me the two of you were coming over here this morning to start doing some work on the house and grounds. I asked if I could come, too, and he said you could use all the help you could get. So here I am. Do you mind?"

Mind? She was still tingling from the shock of pleasure she received when she learned he'd be here, to say nothing of the effect just seeing him had on her. But why would he offer to help when he'd bid her goodbye last week?

"I'm grateful for the assistance," she assured him. "Just so long as you don't feel you have to."

They were still gazing at each other, and his eyes darkened. "Why would I feel that way?"

She shook her head but was careful not to break eye contact. "I don't know. Why would you offer to help if you didn't?"

He put up his hand and gently ran one finger down the side of her face. "Because I miss you like hell when I don't see you."

Before her shaking knees could give out, Shawn's voice broke the magnetism. "Hey, come on, you two. Give me a little help here. I can't carry all this stuff by myself."

They both jumped and rushed to the back of the car where Shawn was gathering up tools.

The rest of the morning was spent going over the property and assessing what needed to be done to qualify it for a bank loan. Since she would be selling it as a fixer-upper, the requirements weren't as stringent as they would have been otherwise. It had to meet the safety code, however, which meant extensive electrical wiring. Also a new front porch and the stairs leading up to it.

The tension between Jodi and Rick had evaporated once they turned their attention to the house, and she enjoyed working with him. He was awfully smart, and very knowledgeable about the construction business. It turned out that he'd not only helped his dad keep the family home in good repair but he'd also worked summers in construction when he was in college, so they were both fairly expert on the subject.

At noon they went home for the lunch Dorothy had cooked for them, then returned to the site and tackled the yard. That proved to be a monumental project, too big for one afternoon. They'd hardly made a dent in it before it began getting dark, and cold, and they were forced to stop.

Dorothy and Shawn insisted that Rick have supper with them, too, so he went to his own house to shower and change while Jodi and Shawn cleaned up at home.

The hot water from the shower felt good on Jodi's tired and knotted muscles. She wasn't used to climbing trees and pushing a lawn mower, not even an electrical one. By the time she'd finally forced herself out from under the shower and dressed in a comfortable long dress with her freshly shampooed auburn hair spilling around her shoulders, Rick had arrived and supper was on the table.

The gleam in Rick's eyes told Jodi he liked the way she looked, but he kept his side of the conversation strictly impersonal as they all discussed their progress on the house, and the work still to be done. By the time they'd finished eating they'd agreed to spend the following day working, too, since Shawn and Rick had to go back to their regular jobs on Monday.

Jodi offered to help Dorothy clean up the kitchen, but she wouldn't hear of it. "You've been working like a Trojan all day, using muscles you probably didn't know you had, and you look worn-out. Go on in the parlor and curl up in front of the television with the men. It won't take but a few minutes to load the dishwasher and then I'll join you."

Jodi didn't argue. Dorothy was right, she *was* exhausted and every muscle in her body hurt. She followed Rick and his dad into the living room, and Rick led her to the long, comfortable sofa. He picked up a decorative pillow and sat down by the thickly upholstered arm at the end, then patted the seat beside him. "Sit here."

She did as he commanded, too tired to argue. The cushions were soft and inviting, but he wasn't content yet. He put the pillow on his lap and issued another order. "Scoot down a little, then stretch out with your head on the pillow."

That got her hackles up. "I can't do that," she said, shocked that he'd suggest it, especially with his parents present.

"Of course you can," he countered. "All I want to do is massage some of those knots out of your muscles. It will help you to relax, and you'll feel much better."

"But...but—"

"What's the matter, don't you trust me?" He sounded hurt. "Mom and Dad are here, for heaven's sake, and they're well experienced as chaperones. Believe me, I know. I could cite chapter and verse."

It sounded reasonable when he put it like that, and she'd welcome anything that would relieve some of her pain. She stole a glance at Shawn in the big recliner, and caught him grinning. "It's all right," he told her. "My son is a licensed masseur. He studied it as an extension of a first-aid course when he was on the Detroit police force. Besides, I'll personally break his hand if it wanders anyplace it shouldn't."

"Don't think he won't, either," Rick muttered. "And if he doesn't, Mom will."

Jodi couldn't resist Shawn's grin, and she chuckled, too. "With such iron-clad guarantees, how can I resist?" She stretched out on her side with her head on the pillow in Rick's lap.

Almost immediately she knew this was a mistake. One could easily become addicted to it. His hands were large but gentle as they rubbed her neck, shoulders and back until he'd relaxed her screaming nerve ends. Then his fingers dug deeper, loosening the tangled sinews and soothing the anxiety she hadn't known she was feeling....

Jodi didn't remember falling asleep, but when she woke the bright early-morning sun was shining. She was still stretched out on the couch, but her head was no longer pillowed in Rick's lap. She was alone and still wearing her dress, but without her shoes. A crocheted afghan had been spread over her.

The grandfather clock chimed seven times, and when it stopped she heard someone running water in the kitchen, probably making coffee. Pushing back the afghan she sat up. She still ached all over, but it was a more manageable soreness than it had been before Rick's massage.

The man was a versatile wonder. At various times he'd been an A student, a masseur, a construction worker, a street cop and chief of police. Not only that, but he was an expert in all of them. Was there anything he couldn't do? She doubted it, and her admiration for him was rapidly becoming boundless.

If she didn't get out of here pretty quick and go back to Ohio, she was going to be in big trouble! The last thing she wanted was to fall in love with a man who didn't love her, and her feelings for Rick grew deeper every time they were together.

She stood and slid her feet into her flat-heeled pumps

arranged neatly on the floor beside the couch. Someone had tucked her in last night, and the suspicion that it might have been Rick nearly undid her. Damn! If he had, she'd have given anything to have been awake to enjoy it.

The aroma of fresh-brewed coffee led her into the kitchen, where she found Dorothy stirring oatmeal. Rick's mom smiled as Jodi yawned and stretched. "What happened last night?" she asked sheepishly. "I don't remember anything after Rick started massaging my back."

"I'm afraid you were totally done in," Dorothy answered. "I was going to wake you up when Rick got ready to leave, but he said not to. He said he had you all relaxed, and to just let you sleep there on the couch. He was the one who took off your shoes and covered you with the afghan. I hope you were warm enough."

Jodi shook her head. "I don't know, but I must have been. I wasn't aware of a thing until I woke up just a few minutes ago."

The rest of the day went much like Saturday, and by the time it was too dark to work at the house any longer they'd made great progress in clearing the property around the house. They'd pruned the trees and bushes that could be saved, made arrangements with a professional to come over in the next few days to cut down the dead ones and had hacked away the overgrown grass and weeds that had destroyed the lawn.

Rick ate supper at his parents' home that evening, too, and afterward Jodi sat with him on the sofa in front of the marble fireplace and watched television with Shawn and Dorothy. Rick didn't suggest another massage, but the touch of his thigh against hers caused her heartbeat to speed up.

They were watching an original made-for-television movie based on the bestselling novel of a popular romance writer, and it was highly emotional, with lots of sexual tension that heated her blood and sent it coursing through her body.

It was affecting Rick, too. She could tell by the way his thigh muscles tightened and his breathing speeded up.

Reluctantly, as though he couldn't help himself, he reached over and took her hand and held it on the top of his leg. It looked innocent enough, especially since the only light was the glow from the fire and his parents were sitting in their easy chairs at the back of the room, but their entwined fingers twitched and tightened when the passion on the screen escalated.

By the time the movie was over, both Jodi and Rick knew it was time for him to make a hasty exit, which he did, leaving them both throbbing with frustrated desire. There was no doubt in Jodi's mind that he wanted her badly, but a few days ago he'd made it plain that his need was strictly physical. He didn't love her and had no intention of marrying her, and she was determined not to get tangled up in such a shallow love affair no matter how attracted she was to him.

The following morning, Jodi dropped by Victor Stuart's law office to pick up her contract.

"There's no legal problems with this," he told her as he handed it to her, "but be careful to make sure the price and other terms of sale are what you agreed to before you sign it."

She took the document and nodded. "I went over it point by point with Farley when I picked it up from him on Friday. He feels I'm pricing the property too high, but he's drawn it up according to my terms. I'll read it over again, but if you say the legalities are fair and agreeable on both sides I'll sign."

Finch Realty was only a couple of blocks from Victor's office, and she headed over there without bothering to call for an appointment. Farley wasn't with a client and welcomed her in. They went over the terms once more, and after warning her again that she was asking too much, he gave her a pen and showed her where to sign.

"Will you put up a For Sale sign right away?" she asked as she handed him back the pen.

He sighed. "I'll send someone over to do it immediately," he said and proceeded to prove it by calling to his secretary. "Get hold of Wally and tell him to put up a sign on the Coldwell property," he ordered when she appeared in the doorway.

She nodded and left, and Farley turned his attention to Jodi again. "Don't expect a quick sale at this price," he repeated. "I understand you've been fixing the place up."

Jodi blinked with surprise. How would he know that? He didn't live anywhere near the area.

"There aren't many secrets in Copper Canyon, are there?" she observed.

"I doubt that there are any." He sounded disgruntled. "So don't do or say anything you don't want the whole town to know. I should think you'd want to wait until you're finished before listing it for sale."

She shook her head firmly. "No. Anyone who is interested will see what we're doing. It should help you sell it."

He grunted. "Don't get your hopes up. You might as well pack up and go back to Ohio. You don't want to sit around here waiting for it to sell at your price."

Jodi stood, said goodbye and left without commenting. There was no sense in arguing with him. She wasn't sure he'd even try to get the amount she wanted, but she wasn't going to back down.

What was the matter with him, anyway? The more he could sell the property for, the more commission he'd make, so why was he so unwilling to even try? Oh, sure, it would take a little more time and effort, but from what she'd observed, real estate wasn't exactly booming in this small town.

* * *

The next morning Jodi drove by her aunt's house to see if the sign had been put up as Farley had promised. It had, although it was partially obscured from the street by one of the scraggly overgrown bushes that were scheduled to be cut down.

Later that evening Shawn, Dorothy and Jodi had just sat down to supper when an ear-piercing siren shattered the peaceful silence with a resonant yowling wail that bounced up and down the decibel scale and was joined by the equally resonant howling of dogs all over the neighborhood.

"What on earth was that?" Jodi asked shakily.

Dorothy and Shawn took it in stride. "It was just the fire alarm," Dorothy explained. "We have a volunteer fire department, and the alarm has to be loud enough to extend to all areas of town and call the firefighters. They don't stay at the fire station the way they do in the city."

"I wonder where the fire is," Jodi mused as she picked up her fork.

"Rick will know," Shawn said. "I'll call him after we finish eating and find out."

They didn't have to wait that long. Not more than five minutes later the phone rang and Dorothy got up to answer it. Since it was in the kitchen her part of the conversation was clearly audible.

"Hello," she said. "Oh, hello, son. We were going to call you in a few minutes..." There was a pause, then she gasped. "Oh my God! No!" Another pause. "Yes, she's right here. Hold on."

She turned to Jodi, and the look on her face made Jodi's blood run cold. "It's Rick," she said unnecessarily. "He wants to talk to you."

Dorothy held out the phone and Jodi grabbed it.

"Rick?" she said breathlessly.

"Jodi," he answered, his tone both urgent and gentle. "I've sent a car for you. I'm sure you'll want to be here."

Her knees shook and she leaned against the wall as he continued. "Sweetheart, your aunt's house is on fire. It's burning out of control, and I'm afraid there's no hope of saving anything."

Chapter Six

Fifteen minutes later the driver of the police car, who had introduced himself to Jodi, Shawn and Dorothy as Clayton, double-parked at the entrance to Red Robin Lane. They'd all been watching the smoke and flames from many blocks away, and up close it was an inferno. Both the house and the closest trees and bushes surrounding it were burning, and the street was cordoned off from all except emergency vehicles.

Jodi watched in silent horror as the flames leapt and roared, belching heavy black smoke into the already suffocating atmosphere and greedily destroying everything they touched. Although it was dark outside, the street was illuminated by the glow of the fire, and she could see the firemen in yellow protective garments shooting gallons of water through oversize hoses into the holocaust.

Fortunately, although it was cold there was only a light breeze. A full-blown wind would have made the situation even more disastrous.

The back door next to Jodi was wrenched open and Rick reached in to take her hand. He must have been standing there watching for them. Without hesitation she scrambled out of the automobile and into his waiting arms. For a moment she couldn't speak. It was enough just to be held by him. Rick would take care of her and make everything right. He wouldn't let this hellish nightmare torment her.

From far away she heard another siren that got louder as it came closer. Rick tensed. "That's the fire department from Grangeville," he said and released her. "This blaze is too wild for our guys to handle alone. I've got to go. Clayton will stay with you. Will you be all right?"

She wanted to scream, *No!* No, she wouldn't be all right. She needed his arms around her, his strength, his soothing voice telling her it was only a bad dream.

But he was already disentangling himself from her, and she knew she had to let him go. She was in no danger, but the firefighters were, and probably some of the neighboring property, as well. Thank God, there were no residents close by. Having a big, strong, loving protector was a beautiful fantasy, but fabrication was a luxury no one could afford in this hell on earth.

She unlocked her arms from around his neck and backed away. "Of course I'll be okay," she said as convincingly as she could. "And you needn't tie up another police officer. Take Clayton with you. I'll look after Dorothy and Shawn. We can talk later."

Rick lowered his head and kissed her forehead. "I knew I could count on you," he said and sprinted down Red Robin Lane toward the fire with Clayton beside him.

Jodi turned back to Shawn and Dorothy and wished she was as sure of herself as Rick was of her.

The surrounding streets were lined with cars driven to the scene by the voyeurs and the curious who for some twisted reason found entertainment in other people's disaster. Rick's troops strove to hold back the crowds while the firefighters battled the fire. His parents and Jodi sat in the police car at the end of the street and watched as Jodi's house was consumed in the blaze.

Finally, after what seemed like hours it was brought under control. The Grangeville fire department left and the Copper Canyon firefighters no longer needed help from the police force. Rick was free to leave.

He bundled them all into his car and took them home, where Dorothy cleared the supper things off the table and made coffee, Shawn mixed more substantial drinks and Jodi wandered around in a confused daze until Rick took her by the arm, led her to the sofa and sat down beside her.

Shawn appeared and handed her a brandy snifter. "Here," he said, "drink this. It'll help you to calm down and think."

She didn't like brandy, but she'd do anything to shake off the fog of desolation that had settled around her. Taking the glass she sipped the liquor, then put her head back against the sofa. "I just don't understand." She sighed. "How did that fire get started? I mean, I know the electrical system in the house was old and needed replacing, but when we were over there working, we didn't touch the wiring. We were mostly busy in the yard."

Rick put his arm under her waist and drew her closer to him so her head rested on his shoulder. "You're right, honey," he said as he settled her comfortably, "and it's not likely that it was an electrical fire."

"Then what?" she asked as she snuggled against him. For some reason it was important to her to know how such a fire could have ignited when there was nobody living there.

Shawn, who had seated himself in one of the lounge chairs, spoke. "Have you talked to the fire chief yet, son?"

"Only briefly," Rick answered. "It's suspicious, that's for sure, but we won't know what set it off until we get some investigators up here from Boise to examine the ruins.

Bob's already put in a call to them. They'll be here first thing tomorrow morning."

Jodi assumed that Bob was the fire chief, but she had a more vital concern right now. "What does 'suspicious' mean?"

"It just means that we haven't been able to determine how the fire started and need someone more knowledgeable to investigate for us," he said quickly.

Rather too quickly, Jodi thought. As though he was holding something back.

"But surely somebody must have an idea about it," she said somewhat querulously.

Rick sighed and squeezed her. "Sure. Everyone in town has a suspicion, and each one is different. We can't investigate something like that in the middle of the night. Tomorrow, when it's daylight, we'll sift through the ashes, look over the grounds and work with the people from Boise. Meanwhile, we have officers stationed there tonight to make sure nobody tampers with the evidence, if there is any."

Jodi felt foolish. Who did she think she was, trying to tell the chief of police how to do his job?

She sat up and reached back to put the empty brandy snifter on the long table behind the couch, then cuddled once more into his embrace. Tonight she needed his warmth and comfort. She'd worry about the consequences tomorrow.

He put both arms around her and held her close. "It's really not as much of a disaster as it seems, Jodi. The house was old and needed a lot of expensive repairs just to bring it up to code. I checked with Lowery from the bank, and he said the building was fully insured. You won't lose financially, and you can still sell the lot."

A twinge of unease shot through her. It wasn't the loss of income that had upset her, but now that Rick mentioned it there was something that troubled her.

She raised her head and looked at him. "Rick, how come you checked on whether or not the house was insured tonight? As busy as you were trying to control the crowd at the site and make sure no one was injured, I'd have thought you'd wait until the bank opened in the morning to inquire about insurance."

He stiffened and looked away from her. "My men and I were investigating the cause of the fire as well as keeping order, so when I saw Lowery among the spectators, I asked him. I'd have had to do it tomorrow anyway, and I thought you'd sleep better tonight if you knew it wasn't going to be a total loss."

"But what if it hadn't been insured?" she prodded.

This time he looked straight at her. "Then I wouldn't have told you until tomorrow."

Now she felt like an ungrateful brat. He was only trying to make the whole thing easier for her, and she'd jumped to all the wrong conclusions.

She groaned and buried her face in his neck. "I'm sorry," she murmured urgently. "I don't know what's gotten into me. You've been so thoughtful and caring ever since I first met you, and here I am practically accusing you of...of..."

"Of what, Jodi?" She heard the hurt in his tone and felt even worse. "What is it you're accusing me of?"

"I...I don't know," she sobbed as her control snapped and the tears she'd been fighting all evening streamed down her cheeks. She collapsed against him and let them fall.

His arms tightened around her. "It's okay. Don't cry. You're right to be suspicious of strangers."

That made her cry all the harder. He wasn't a stranger. He was the man she loved, but she couldn't tell him that! If she did, he'd not only feel more responsible for her, but he'd pity her as well and that was the last thing she wanted from him.

"You...you're not a stranger," she stammered. "You're

my dear friend, and I really wasn't accusing you of anything."

Again she raised her head and looked at him. "I don't know what I was doing. I can't seem to think straight. This has all been such a shock."

He kissed her tearstained wet cheeks. "Of course it has. Do you want me to call Dr. Sam? He'd give you a sedative—"

"No!" she interrupted. "I'm not going to wake up a doctor in the middle of the night. If you don't mind holding me for a few more minutes, I'll be okay."

He guided her head back down on his shoulder. "There's nothing I'd rather do than hold you," he assured her tenderly. "Just go ahead and cry if it makes you feel better."

Oh, she was feeling better all right, but it wasn't the crying that was comforting her. It was Rick's arms sheltering her, his breath warm and fresh on her cheek, and his hands gently massaging her back. She didn't even dare think about the way his long, lean body felt pressed against her own, making her ache to caress him, too.

A few minutes later Dorothy came in with a tray of filled coffee mugs, and Jodi reluctantly straightened up, pulled away from Rick and dried her eyes with the heels of her palms. She was a big girl now and it was time to quit acting like a child. She had to stop depending on other people for her well-being and start taking care of herself again.

She'd been independent for a long time, and she liked it that way, but it would be so easy to fall under the spell of the close-knit McBride family.

That could be a mistake of heartbreaking proportions!

On the following day the fire was the prime topic of conversation all over town. By now everybody knew that Jodi was Aretha Coldwell's niece and sole heir, and people stopped Dorothy and her in the supermarket, the beauty shop and the gas station to get all the latest information.

Shawn was also accosted at work and on the street everywhere he went since it was common knowledge that Jodi was staying with him and Dorothy. Even the owner of the *Copper Canyon Star Journal,* the small town's weekly newspaper, called to conduct a telephone interview with her. All she could tell him was that she didn't know any more about what caused it than he did.

At noon Rick phoned to say that the investigators from Boise wanted to talk with her, and could she come to the police station at two o'clock? The call troubled her. She'd been treated like a celebrity all morning by the gossip hungry townspeople, but now she detected an ominous ring in Rick's tone that made her feel like a criminal being called to answer for her crime.

Determined to make a good impression on those men from the State Department of Fire Investigators, or whatever the heck it was called, she showered and started dressing all over again. She applied makeup with special care, then selected a gray wool tailored suit that was actually too sophisticated for a small town, although it was just right for a businesswoman in Cincinnati. Also, it flattered her auburn hair. If they thought she was just a naive country maiden who could be intimidated by their city ways she intended them to know just by looking at her that Cincinnati was many times larger and more urbane than Boise.

She timed it so she arrived at the police station, parked her car and walked into the building at exactly two o'clock.

She was immediately ushered into Rick's office, where he and two other men were sitting at the desk. They all three stood, and she saw a look of admiration in their expressions, and smiled. Apparently the suit had been a good choice.

Rick introduced the two investigators as Don and Neal. They had last names but she didn't catch them. They were both tall and probably in their late thirties, but Don was blond and Neal was dark. Someone produced another chair, and they all crowded around the desk, with her sitting behind it next to Rick and the other two in front.

She was grateful to him for putting her beside him. She'd never been interrogated before and the experience was unsettling. She wasn't even sure why these men wanted to interview her. She was a stranger in town and knew absolutely nothing about the fire.

Rick cleared his throat. "Ron, Neal and I have been all over your property this morning, Jodi, and we've come to an indisputable conclusion."

He paused and she felt a chill of foreboding. "The fire last night was not caused by faulty wiring or carelessness. It was arson. Someone set it deliberately."

She felt as if the breath had been knocked out of her. Arson! Someone had deliberately started that fire that wreaked such havoc and could have easily resulted in injuries? Even fatalities!

"No!" The word sounded as if it had been squeezed out of her, like an accordion.

"There's no doubt about it." Rick's tone was soothing, but what he was telling her was onerous.

She tried to take a deep breath, but it turned out shallow at best. "But why? How can you be so sure it wasn't an accident?"

"It was set with a flammable liquid," he explained, "and whoever did it overdid it, so to speak. The place was saturated. That's why it went up in flames so fast and got out of control so quickly. We can't figure out how the arsonist got out of there without being burned once he lit the match or whatever was used to ignite it. We've found no identifiable remains of a body, but we've sent for a team of experts on that, too."

Jodi blinked. The horrors just kept multiplying. "You mean you think someone died in that inferno?"

Rick shook his head. "We have no idea, but it's possible.

That will be up to the other state investigators from Boise to determine."

She sank back in the chair and tried to get a grip on herself. This whole conversation wasn't making any sense.

"Why would anyone want to burn down that old house?" she asked wearily. "It was an eyesore for sure, but we'd been working at fixing it up." She grimaced. "The way news gets around this town, everyone must have known I was trying to sell it as a fixer-upper to a family who would do just that."

For the first time one of the other two men spoke. "We understand the house was fully insured," Neal said.

Rick sent him a dirty look, but for a moment Jodi was bewildered. "Well, yes, I guess it was. I—"

Then it hit her, and her eyes widened as her mouth dropped open. "You think *I* set the fire to collect the insurance?" she cried, her voice rough with shock.

"It's a possibility," Neal said as Rick sprang to his feet.

"No!" he shouted and glared at the investigators. "And I'll remind you two that this is my jurisdiction. You're here to help the fire department find out the cause of the fire, and you've done that. My office is responsible for finding the arsonist."

Both men stood also. "Yeah, well, you'd better rescue yourself, fellah, because it's obvious that you can't be impartial where this suspect is concerned," Don said acidly.

"Jodi is not a suspect," Rick denied angrily. "She has an airtight alibi. She was with my mother all day yesterday, and at the time the fire broke out she was having supper with my parents at their home, so watch what you're accusing her of. Sounds to me like you're coming dangerously close to giving her grounds for a lawsuit."

The men grumbled but sat back down. So did Rick. "Now then," he said and settled back in his chair. "Do you have anything *relevant* to question Ms. Hopkins about?"

"Yes, we do," Neal snapped.

Rick looked at Jodi. "Are you willing to answer their questions?" he asked softly.

Jodi had been badly shaken by the implication that she'd set fire to her own house, but she'd managed to pull herself together again while Rick, bless his heart, was defending her. He was right. She did have an alibi. A fact she'd forgotten in the shock of being accused.

"Only if I can have a lawyer present," she answered firmly, determined not to take any more abuse from the lunkheads.

"That won't be necessary," Don assured her. "You're not under arrest."

She could see that they were daunted by her threat to bring in an attorney. "That's right, I'm not, and I don't intend to be. I'm not answering any more questions without counsel."

They looked at each other and Don uttered a muffled oath. "In that case we'll postpone it until later," he said, and they both got up and left.

Jodi breathed a sigh of relief and realized that she was trembling. "Whew," she said as she rubbed her sweaty palms over her skirt.

"Honey, I'm sorry," Rick apologized. "I had no idea they were going to pull something like that or I'd never have agreed to let them interview you."

"I know," she assured him, "but why would they think I'd set fire to my own house?"

He stood. "Unfortunately people sometimes torch their own buildings in hopes of collecting the insurance. Not many of them are smart enough to get away with it, but that doesn't keep them from trying."

He reached his hands down to her in the chair beside him and pulled her up, too. They were standing chest to chest but barely touching.

"You don't believe I'd do something like that, do you?" It was almost a whisper.

His eyes darkened as they searched hers. "I know you wouldn't," he murmured softly just before their lips brushed, then brushed again before he stepped back.

She knew that if she'd sway toward him he'd give her what she so desperately desired, his mouth caressing hers, parting her lips to taste her with his tongue...

With a blink of her eyes she broke the spell and turned her head.

Cool it, Jodi. He's not going to refuse what you offer, but neither will he make promises he has no intention of keeping. Be sure you can handle a short, intense affair before you get involved.

She knew her own advice was good and hoped she was strong enough to obey it.

Rick's voice broke into her introspection. "Jodi, since you're the new owner of the house and I'm the chief of police, I do have to question you. Do you want to do it now or put it off until another time? I know those two clowns upset you—"

She waved her hand in dismissal. "No, I'm all right. Let's do it now and get it over with."

They both sat back down, and he took a tape recorder from a drawer and put it on top of the desk. "Do you mind if I tape our interview?"

She did. For some reason, having her words recorded in a criminal case frightened her, but she knew it had to be done. "No, I don't mind. I have nothing to hide."

Rick spoke into the box, giving the date, time and place as well as both their names, then looked at her. "Now, Jodi, for the record, tell me how you came into possession of the Coldwell property?"

She spoke into the pesky recorder of the circumstances surrounding her inheritance and her reason for being in Copper Canyon. It was a well-rehearsed story since she'd told it many times to the people she'd met since coming here, and she soon forgot that she was talking into a microphone.

When she finished, Rick had another question. "Can you think of any reason why someone would want to burn down your great-aunt's house?"

She shook her head. "No. I told you, I've had no contact with her since I was a small child. I didn't know her at all. As far as I can tell she was my last living relative on my father's side, and she and my mother didn't keep in touch."

Rick nodded. "All right, now, do you know of a reason why anybody would want to damage *your* property."

Jodi's eyes widened. Dear God! It hadn't occurred to her that someone might be out to get *her!*

"No! I don't see how that's possible." She sounded as dumbfounded as she felt. "I've only been here a couple of weeks, and everyone I've met has been so friendly. Surely you don't think—"

"I don't think anything, Jodi," he said. "I'm simply asking questions that need to be answered. There's nothing personal about this, so please don't be upset. Can you tell me about your business dealings with Finch Realty? I understand you recently placed the property you inherited for sale with them."

Thoughtfully she recounted her conversations with Farley Finch, and also Harlan Lowery. "I signed the contract yesterday," she concluded, "and Mr. Finch had a For Sale sign placed on the property. I drove by and saw it yesterday afternoon."

Rick looked straight at her. "So is the fire going to represent a good-sized financial loss to you?"

She caught her breath. Why was he asking that? He already knew the answer. He also knew the subject of insurance was one she didn't want to discuss now that she knew it could incriminate her. Dammit, she'd trusted him, and now he'd betrayed her.

"Turn off the tape recorder," she snapped, not bothering to be polite.

He nodded and pushed the button.

"Damn you, Rick," she raged. "Are you trying to trick me? If so, I'm not as stupid as you seem to think. There will be no more interview until I have a lawyer present."

Rick didn't look surprised, just sad. "I'm sorry if you think I'd trick you, honey. I know you had nothing to do with setting the fire, but I need you to answer my questions for the record. Do you want to call Victor Stuart?"

Without waiting for an answer, he pushed the telephone across the desk to her.

She picked it up, and Rick told her the number to punch. Vic answered the phone himself.

"Victor, this is Jodi Hopkins," she said.

"Oh, hi, Jodi," he answered. "Hey, I'm sorry to hear about the fire. Are you all right?"

"No, I'm not," she said testily. "There are some investigators here from Boise who seem to think I set the fire in order to collect the insurance."

Victor swore. "Where are you?"

"I'm at the police station. The investigators left, but Rick wants to question me, and I'm not answering anything more until you can be here."

"Good girl," he said. "I'll be over in about ten minutes." He hung up and so did she.

"He'll be here in a few minutes," she told Rick.

"Good," he said. "None of my officers are going to try to make you say anything you don't want to. I'll see to that, but you do have to answer the questions, Jodi. Either here or in the district attorney's office, and I have no control over them. I'm sorry those goons from the state upset you, but I'm relieved that Victor will be representing you. He'll see to it that no one in any law enforcement agency violates your civil rights."

Jodi was ashamed of accusing Rick of trying to trick her

into answering questions she didn't want to. "I'm sorry, too, Rick," she said haltingly. "I know you wouldn't do anything to hurt me, but I'm just so scared. I can't believe someone would think I'd do anything so monstrous as to deliberately set a fire..." She choked on a sob.

He got up and walked around the desk to hunker down beside her chair. "I understand, sweetheart," he said and took her clasped hands in his. "This whole thing is a nasty business. I don't believe for a minute that you had anything to do with it, but I'm sure as hell going to find out who did. That means I have to interview you. I'd be derelict in my duty if I didn't, and any show of partiality for you by me would go harder on you, too."

He brought her hands to his mouth and kissed them. "I'll ask the questions, and you let Victor tell you which ones to answer. Okay?"

Her lips quivered, although she managed a small smile. "Okay, but I really do trust you, Rick."

The attorney arrived a few minutes later, and from then on everything went smoothly. Vic refused to let her answer any questions about insurance, explaining that she had no firsthand knowledge of the subject.

When it was over Jodi felt drained. "This is all so confusing," she said to Rick as she slumped back in her chair. "I have an airtight alibi for the time the blaze was set, so why do you keep coming back to the subject of insurance? Surely you believe your own parents. They've told you I was at home with them for a couple of hours before the fire started, and you know I was there when you called. You talked to me."

"It's just routine—" Rick started to say, but he was cut off by Victor.

"No, don't be evasive," he interrupted. "She has to be made aware of what she's facing, Rick. It's the only way she can defend herself."

He turned his attention to Jodi. "I'm sorry to have to tell

you this, but just because you didn't set the fire doesn't mean you aren't responsible for it.''

She blinked, and her mind went blank. What on earth was he getting at?

He took a deep breath and got right to the point. ''You could have conceived the idea and paid someone else to do it.''

Chapter Seven

Jodi stared at the attorney in stunned incomprehension. Surely Victor didn't believe that! He was her lawyer, for heaven's sake. He was suppose to be on her side.

"That's a...a monstrous thing to say!" Her voice shook with agitation.

She looked from one man to the other. "How could you possibly believe..." Her words trailed off as she realized that Rick hadn't come to her defense the way he had a few minutes ago.

"Both of you!" The words exploded from deep inside her. "You both believe I arranged to have someone set that fire—"

"Calm down, Jodi," Victor said as Rick stood and walked around the desk to stand behind her and put his hands on her shoulders.

"You've got it all wrong, sweetheart," Rick told her and gently pulled her back so that her head rested against his chest.

"Neither of us believes that you had anything to do with torching that house," Victor said emphatically, "but it's vital that you know and understand the way the investigators can and will look at it. As of now you're the only one we've been able to find who stands to profit from that fire. Also, you're the beautiful and sophisticated stranger from the big city in a small town. Ergo a natural suspect before you even do anything."

"That's not fair!" she said, outraged.

"Of course it's not," Victor agreed, "but who said life was fair?"

"But I didn't even know the house was insured," she insisted.

"We know that," Rick said as his talented fingers caressed her shoulders, "but it's a difficult thing to prove."

"But you were the one who told me," she reminded him.

"I know, and I believe you when you say you didn't know it till then, but we need more than just your word for it. We need proof, and that's hard to come by."

The more they talked, the more deeply Jodi felt herself being mired in what had proven to be a major crime. She wasn't just frightened, she was terrified!

"Isn't there something in the constitution about being innocent until proven guilty?" she asked tartly.

"Yes, there is," Victor said, "but the prosecution only has to prove guilt *beyond a reasonable doubt.* People are convicted on circumstantial evidence all the time, so the stronger our defense the better."

Her small surge of rebellion died. "Are...are you going to arrest me?" she stammered, and realized she was trembling.

Rick groaned and crossed his arms across her collarbone as he tipped his head down to nuzzle her hair. "No! It's not going to come to that. There's not enough evidence to charge you."

Victor spoke up. "Just remember, don't talk to anybody, not even Rick, about the fire without me present."

* * *

When Victor and Jodi left the police station they went over to the bank to talk to Harlan Lowery as executor of the Coldwell estate. He was free and welcomed them into his office.

"Jodi, I'm so sorry about that awful fire at your house." Harlan said as they all took seats at the desk. "Have you any idea what started it?"

She kept quiet and let Victor answer. "We don't have much information yet, and that's why we're here. As Jodi's lawyer I'd like to see a copy of the fire insurance policy on the house."

Harlan looked surprised. "Yes, of course, I'll get it."

He left the room, then returned in a few minutes with a file folder and sat back down at the desk. "Here you are," he said, removing a document from the file and handing it to the attorney.

"Mr. Lowery, why didn't you tell me the house was insured?" Jodi asked.

Harlan's eyes widened. "But I did, my dear."

A bolt of shock ripped through her, and she saw Victor look at her and frown. "No, you did not!" she said angrily.

"I must have, Jodi," he insisted. "I went over all the papers relevant to your aunt's estate with you. And even if I had missed that policy, you have a copy of it. I gave you copies of everything in this file. Don't you remember?"

Yes, now she did remember. He'd gone over a lot of papers with her, but she was sure there'd been no mention of fire insurance on the house. She also remembered that he'd had copies made of everything and gave them to her in a folder, which he slipped into a brown manila envelope. She'd taken it home, tossed it in her suitcase and never gave it another thought.

Oh, damn! Was it possible there was a copy of the policy in that folder? If so, she'd never be able to convince anybody that she hadn't known about it!

"Y-yes, I do remember now," she admitted, "but

haven't even opened that envelope since you gave it to me, and I have no memory of any mention of fire insurance.''

Victor was scanning the insurance policy and frowning. ''It looks to me as if the house was overinsured,'' he said to Harlan. ''Neither your estimate nor the independent one Jodi had done listed the value this high.''

Now Harlan frowned. ''Let me see,'' he said and picked up the policy Victor slid across the big mahogany desk at him.

''Hmm,'' he murmured as he read. ''Yes, I see what you mean. It's easy to understand, however. This policy was taken out many years ago, when both the area and the property were in much better shape. Surely you remember, Victor. Back in the sixties that part of town was choice property. Those old homes were still in prime condition then, and some of our leading citizens lived there.''

Victor still looked puzzled, and Harlan leaned back in his chair and locked his fingers across his still-flat stomach. ''No, you probably wouldn't remember. You were too young then, but it wasn't until the focus of the residential area shifted from the east to the north side of town where there was plenty of room to expand that the Red Robin Lane area began to deteriorate.''

He tapped his pencil on the desk. ''Aretha Coldwell was a stubborn old lady who refused to relocate. Said that place had been owned by her family since the turn of the century and she wasn't going to be forced out. She so seldom left the house or had contact with the outside world that she probably didn't realize that property values had tumbled. It's a shame, too, because she was paying more in premiums than was necessary or advisable.''

''Then why didn't the bank take some action?'' Jodi demanded. It looked to her as if they'd been grossly negligent. ''You were managing her financial affairs, weren't you?''

Harlan straightened up and looked at her sternly. ''We paid her bills and handled her investments, and now that she's dead we're her executors. However, while she was alive and supposedly of sound mind, it was not our place to tell her how to spend her money except for the amount she asked us to invest for her each month.''

''*Was* she of sound mind?'' Victor asked.

''I have no idea,'' Harlan said crisply. ''If there had been any doubt about it, that would have been up to her family—'' he nodded toward Jodi ''—and possibly her doctor to determine.''

A combination of guilt and anger left Jodi seething. ''If you mean me,'' she grated, ''I didn't even know she existed. Apparently the only time I ever saw her was at my father's funeral when I was six years old, and I don't remember that.''

''That may be,'' Harlan said smugly, ''but don't blame me, either. As long as she was alive and no danger to herself or anyone else, the bank's sole function was to pay her bills as they came to us and handle her investments.''

''Now come on, you two,'' Victor interrupted as he held up his hands for silence. ''No one's accusing anybody of anything. We're just trying to get to the bottom of this thing. Jodi, do you still insist that you knew nothing about this insurance policy?''

She nodded emphatically. ''Yes, I do. I admit I should have gone over those papers he gave me and familiarize myself with them, but I do not remember him telling me anything about insurance on the house or on anything else.''

''Maybe this will teach you to listen more closely next time you're being informed of something,'' Harlan scolded.

''Oh, knock it off, Lowery,'' Victor said as he stood. ''When was the last time you went over your insurance policies and other important papers?''

''Once a year,'' he boasted with a smirk, ''and again when anything comes up for renewal.''

Victor took Jodi's hand and pulled her up beside him.

"Yeah, well, that figures," he muttered and led her out of the room.

Outside it was getting dark, and the chilly breeze had turned to a cold wind that blew right through Jodi's suit coat and made her shiver. The gathering clouds were dark and threatened snow.

They walked briskly to her car, and Victor opened the door so she could slide in under the steering wheel. "As soon as you get back to the McBrides', check and see if you have that policy," he instructed her. "If you do, don't tell anybody about it, not even Rick or his parents, and I'll pick you up in the morning and take you to the police station where you can amend your statement."

"But why can't we do that now?" she asked. She didn't want to lie to Rick or his parents, not even by omission.

"Because it's getting late and Rick is probably no longer on duty. Also, I have another appointment before I can go home for supper, and Yvonne likes to have meals on time."

"Yvonne?"

"My wife," he said with a grin. "We have two sons age six and four, and eight-month-old twin girls. Plus, Yvonne runs her own business, a clothing boutique. The only way she can keep up with everything is to have a schedule and stick to it as much as possible."

Jodi felt her frustration melt. "What a wonderful family," she said enviously. "You must feel truly blessed."

He laughed. "Usually," he admitted. "Then again... well, you have to live it to believe it. Call me first thing in the morning," he said and closed the door.

The next morning Jodi and Victor arranged to meet at the police station at ten o'clock to change her statement about the insurance. Although it hadn't started to snow as forecast, it was cloudy, windy and cold, and Jodi dressed warmly in black wool slacks and a black cable knit pullover sweater under her parka.

She hadn't seen or talked to Rick since she'd left his office the day before, but she had found a copy of the fire insurance policy in with the papers Harlan had given her. How could she have missed it?

There had been a lot of records to go over, and business practices to try to understand. Her mind had been reeling when they'd finished, but she was still sure that the insurance had never been mentioned. She'd read the policy through cover to cover last night and none of it sounded familiar.

It was as if she were on a merry-go-round where each turn plunged her more deeply into jeopardy!

Rick tapped his pen on the desk and stared at the clock on the wall. It said five minutes to ten, and for the past hour and a half he'd been stewing. He hadn't been here when Victor called to make an appointment for him to bring Jodi in, and he wouldn't tell Evelyn, the dispatcher who also acted as part-time secretary since there weren't all that many crimes to dispatch, why they wanted to talk to him.

Rick hadn't seen either of them since they'd left his office yesterday to keep an appointment with Harlan at the bank. Had something gone wrong?

But how could it? He was convinced that Jodi didn't know anything about the fire. He'd heard the shock in her voice when he'd told her about it on the phone, and saw the look on her face when she arrived at the scene and saw it for herself. It was pure horror, and she wasn't a good enough actress to fake it.

At least he didn't think she was.

His stomach roiled, and he realized that he was sweating even though it wasn't overly warm in here. Dammit, he really didn't know her well enough to decide whether she was capable of lying so convincingly or not!

She seemed so sweet, and sort of naive, and she touched

his heart in a way no other woman ever had. But, of course, that was the problem. Was he so involved with her emotionally that his judgment was clouded?

God, he hoped not! That's exactly what he'd been trying to avoid ever since she first walked in here and set his heart pounding. He'd known she was a powerful threat to his future peace of mind—and body.

Like now. Just thinking about her aroused him. He'd tried telling himself it was just a physical reaction that was normal in a more or less celibate male, but deep down he knew better. He wanted to take care of her, protect her and also to know she was there for him when he needed her.

What he needed was a wife, and she was probably the only single woman in town who was strictly off-limits!

A tap on the door startled him out of his reverie, and he looked up to see Victor and Jodi through the glass. He stood and called for them to come in, then came around the desk to shake hands with Victor and say hello to Jodi.

"Let me take your coats," he said and helped Jodi out of her parka, then took Victor's overcoat and hung the garments on the hooks on the wall.

The sight of Jodi nearly took his breath away. She looked irresistible in black. It complimented her vibrant auburn hair and highlighted her hauntingly beautiful blue eyes. He had a difficult time keeping both his gaze and his hands off her.

"What can I do for you two?" he asked after they'd all taken seats.

He noticed that she sent Victor a pleading look just before he answered. "I'm afraid there's been a mix-up and Jodi would like to amend her statement."

Rick felt the long talons of fear clutch at his throat. "I see." His tone sounded raspy. "What part would she like to change?" He couldn't look at her, afraid she'd see the alarm in his eyes.

It was she who answered this time, and now her distress

was plainly visible. "I've come across some information that I think you should be made aware of," she said anxiously.

"What is it, Jodi?" he asked carefully, praying she wasn't going to confess to something he didn't want to know.

"It...it's about the fire insurance on aunt Aretha's house," she stammered, and he had trouble stifling a groan. What was the matter with Victor? Why didn't he shut her up?

Rick held up his hand to stop her. "Just a minute," he commanded and looked at the attorney. "Victor? Aren't you going to advise her on this?"

He shook his head. "I already have. I've advised her to bring it to your attention. If she doesn't, it could be even more harmful to her."

Rick profoundly wished that he'd stayed in Detroit where he didn't know the people he arrested.

He nodded and looked at Jodi. "In that case you'd better tell me."

"I swear I don't remember it," she said urgently, "but Mr. Lowery insists that he went over the policy with me the day after I got here when he was explaining to me about the estate."

Rick was almost sure his heart stopped beating, but before he could catch his breath she continued. "Also, he gave me copies of all the papers we'd reviewed, and last evening when I went through them I found a copy of the fire insurance policy."

Rick closed his eyes and muttered a silent oath. Dear Lord, there was no way he could protect her after an admission like that! He was bound by law to take it down and give it to the district attorney. Her so-called airtight alibi wouldn't be worth a damn if they decided to prosecute her on a charge of paying someone else to set the fire!

He felt sick, and for the first time he wished he'd never gone into law enforcement.

"Jodi, weren't you paying attention when Harlan explained the intricacies of the estate with you?" His voice sounded scratchy, and it was little wonder. He was talking around a giant obstruction in his throat. Probably a suppressed scream of frustration.

"Yes, I was," she said firmly, "and I know that I never saw that policy until yesterday when I opened the envelope he gave me containing copies of the papers we'd discussed. I found it among them."

She shifted nervously in her chair. "Wh-what are you going to do now? Are you...that is, are you going to arrest me this time?"

The very idea was unbearable, and Rick had to restrain himself from going to her, taking her in his arms and assuring her she had nothing to worry about. He ached to comfort her, but he couldn't. It was possible he'd have to arrest her eventually, and if his feelings for her were made known, the prosecution would insist that he be taken off the case. If that happened, he couldn't help her at all!

"No, Jodi, I'm not going to arrest you," he said and hoped she'd pick up on the empathy and tenderness in his tone. "But we will have to revise your statement."

He pushed back his chair and stood. "I'll send Evelyn in to take it down. Victor will be here to advise you, so listen to him, and don't say anything he doesn't want you to. When you're finished you'll be free to go."

It took more than an hour before the document was revised to Jodi's and Victor's satisfaction, typed up and signed, and Rick was nowhere in sight when they left the station. Jodi went back to the McBride home to have dinner with Shawn and Dorothy and tell them all that had happened since yesterday.

She was in tears again by the time she finished the story.

Dorothy got out of her chair and went over to put her arms around Jodi while Shawn took her hand and squeezed it.

"There, there," Dorothy said and handed her a tissue. "Don't be so upset. I know how scared you must be, but Rick and Victor will sort it all out."

She puffed up indignantly. "The very idea. How could anyone think you'd want to burn your own house down?"

"I wouldn't be too concerned if I were you," Shawn said. "The district attorney and I went to school together. He's an intelligent man. It's not likely he'll charge you with anything, but if he seems inclined to, I'll have a talk with him. He knows I wouldn't steer him wrong."

"That's very kind of you," Jodi sobbed as she blew her nose, "but I don't see how I can defend myself. I have no proof that I didn't pay somebody to do it, although I don't know why anyone would think I'd want to. I don't need the money."

"There's no proof that you did do it, either," Shawn reminded her, "and they can't charge you without convincing evidence that you did." He paused. "Did you say you don't need the money?"

She dried her eyes and looked at them. "I don't. Honestly. Aunt Aretha left me enough in investments to live on the interest without working if I don't want to."

Shawn and Dorothy both looked surprised. "Does anyone know this?" Shawn asked.

Jodi shook her head. "Only Harlan Lowery, the executor of the estate. I asked him not to tell anybody. I..." She stopped and managed a tiny smile. "I was embarrassed. I'd never dreamed I'd ever have that much money. I didn't want people to think I was...well...stuck up about it."

"You mean neither Rick nor Victor questioned you about your financial situation?" Dorothy asked.

"No."

Shawn uttered a full throated laugh. "Then it's time you volunteered the information," he said with relief. "My

God, girl, that little 'embarrassing' fact shoots any motive you could have had all to hell!"

Jodi felt like a ton of rocks had been lifted off her slender shoulders, and a happy smile appeared unsummoned. "Are you sure?" She was afraid to believe it.

"As sure as a layman can be about matters of the law, but the best way to check is to call both Rick and Victor and ask them. Better yet, ask them to come over here and then tell them both together face-to-face."

Jodi was rapidly getting into the spirit of it. "You're sure you wouldn't mind?"

"Of course not," Dorothy said. "In fact, I'll do the calling. That is, if you want me to." She grinned. "It'll sound more commanding that way."

"Please do," Jodi said, "and don't take no for an answer."

Dorothy made the calls, and Rick agreed immediately. There was a problem with Victor, though. He hadn't returned to his office after dinner but was home wrestling with baby-sitting problems.

"I'd love to come," he told Dorothy, "but our babysitter went home sick at noon so I have to stay here with the kids. Yvonne can't get away from the boutique because they're having a fashion show this afternoon."

He paused for a moment, then continued. "Any chance you all could come over here? The kids will be taking their naps."

Dorothy happily accepted the invitation, and within half an hour they were all gathered at the Stuarts' home. It was a two-story house in the new subdivision north of town, and as neat and pretty on the inside as the outside.

"I love your house," Jodi said as Victor took her coat.

"Thanks," he said. "So do we. We bought it after the twins were born. We needed more space to spread out in."

"Where are the children?" she asked. "I'd love to see them."

Victor smiled proudly. "Jason, the oldest, is in school, and the other three are taking their naps, but they'll no doubt be up before you leave."

They all congregated in the spacious living room, and Jodi got right to the point. She told them how much she'd inherited from her late aunt's estate, and why she hadn't mentioned it before.

"At first it sounded too much like bragging," she explained, "and later I had no idea it would be relevant in this business about the fire. Will it make a difference, do you think?" She looked from Victor to Rick.

"I should certainly think so," Victor said.

"It definitely will," Rick assured her. "It pretty well wipes out any obvious motive you could have had. Hiring an arsonist would have been expensive, so you wouldn't have profited all that much from it, anyway. If you didn't even need the money, it wouldn't have made any sense to try to defraud the insurance company. Am I right, Victor?"

The attorney nodded in agreement. "You sure are. Since the fire was started under suspicious circumstances, she wouldn't get a settlement from them without a court fight, and that would likely wipe out whatever profit she'd have made even if she won."

His eyes twinkled as he looked straight at her. "I think you're home free, Jodi!"

She felt as if she'd just been released from prison, even though she'd never set foot in one. "Oh, I don't know how I can ever thank all of you," she said breathlessly as a huge smile of relief left her light-headed.

Rick stood and walked to the chair where she was sitting, then reached down to take her hands. "How about starting with a hug for each of us," he said and pulled her up into his arms.

They held each other tightly, sending a rush of hormones to comingle with the adrenaline that was already surging through Jodi, and she finally had to force herself to pull away from him. He let her go reluctantly with a murmured, "I'll be back for more later," and she made the rounds of Shawn, Dorothy and finally Victor. They all hugged her close, and voiced their pleasure that she was no longer under the black cloud of suspicion.

When she got back to Rick he reached out and gathered her to him again without apology or embarrassment.

"How about some coffee?" Victor said. "It's all ready. I even found a couple of boxes of Girl Scout cookies in the cupboard. If you'll just follow me into the dining room..."

With wide grins Dorothy and Shawn followed him out of the room, and Rick nuzzled the sensitive space behind Jodi's ear. "Victor's what's known as a real pal," he murmured and nibbled on her lobe, sending tickles down her spine.

She thought so, too, but was too enchanted to say anything. Instead, she tipped her head to give him room to nuzzle further while she ran her palms over his back. It was covered only with the light blue shirt of his uniform, and she could feel his muscles twitch and fleck.

"Jodi...you've cast...a spell...over me," he said in short gasps between placing kisses on the side of her neck. "I can't get you out of my mind. I've been going crazy with fear for you since the fire."

She put her arms around his neck and blew gently into his ear. He groaned and tightened his arms around her waist. "Everything will be all right now," she whispered. "Would it be breaking any rules if I kissed you?"

She didn't have to wait for an answer. He turned his head and captured her mouth all in one movement. The hormones and adrenaline ignited and sent tongues of fire to heat her blood and set it to racing.

All Rick's common sense shattered as their lips met and clung. Her breath was sweet, her body soft and pliant and her scent an aphrodisiac that tormented his already aching loins and threatened to melt what little self-control he had left.

Mindlessly he placed his hands on her derriere and pushed her pelvis against his throbbing groin, sending tremors all through him and heightening his urgent need. "Oh, Jodi," he moaned against her open mouth. "I want you."

"And I want you," she whispered and gently nibbled at his lower lip, "but this is neither the time nor the place."

The painful truth of that statement brought him down to earth with a thump, although it did little to cool off his libido.

"I know," he rasped as he unlocked her arms from around his neck and peeled himself away from her. "I'm sorry, but once I had you in my arms I...I simply lost control. I'll try not to let it happen again."

She looked hurt. "Are you apologizing?"

Carefully he touched her cheek. "Only for the timing."

Before she could answer, a shrill cry came from somewhere upstairs, followed immediately by another one.

"Uh-oh," Victor's voice sounded from the dining room. "The twins are awake." He came dashing through the living room on his way to the staircase.

"May I help?" Jodi called to him.

"Sure," he answered without breaking stride. "I can use all the help I can get."

He hit the stairs, and Jodi ran to keep up.

Rick went into the dining room and poured himself a cup of coffee, then sat down at the table with his parents. A few minutes later Victor and Jodi appeared, each carrying a tousled, sleepy-eyed infant.

Rick felt a tug at his heart. They were cute little girls, blond with sparkling blue eyes and dressed in red denim overalls and matching red-and-white knit shirts. No wonder Victor was so proud of them. Any man would be!

He tore his thoughts away from Victor's paternal pride and looked at Jodi. She was positively beaming as she hugged the child she was carrying close to her. Both adults sat down and gave the little ones each a cookie which they immediately tried to crumble into their mouths, spilling saliva-wet crumbs down the front of them. Part of the mess landed on Jodi's obviously expensive black slacks and sweater, but she didn't miss a beat, just picked up a napkin and gently wiped the unappetizing garbage off the kid's grinning mouth and ignored her clothes.

"Hey, Bonny," she crooned as she chucked the youngster under her double chin. "You'd have better luck if you didn't try to cram that cookie in your mouth all at once."

Bonny chuckled uproariously and her chubby little hand latched on to Jodi's heavy silver cross pendant with the large pearllike settings and stuck it in her mouth, along with what was left of the cookie goo. Jodi rescued it and gave her a spoon instead, which she started pounding the table with.

Jodi just laughed and hugged her as she blew on the back of the child's neck, making her pound all the harder.

Rick watched from a gray cloud of despair. Jodi was so patient and loving with the kid. She didn't scold or become upset because she'd have to take her clothes to the cleaners. She just distracted the baby with something else while laughing and talking to her.

She obviously hadn't been exaggerating when she said she loved children. That was plainly evident from just seeing her with them. She was a born mother, and she'd never be happy with just a husband and a career.

He closed his eyes, fighting to shut out his misery.

No, Jodi needed babies like an artist needs paints, or a musician needs music. What she most especially didn't need was a husband who would never give them to her. She'd be miserable, and no matter how valiantly she fought against it she'd eventually ask for a divorce.

That would destroy him! It was imperative that he suppress his growing passion for her before it got out of control and ended in disaster.

Chapter Eight

On Monday morning Jodi woke to sunshine and a sense of purpose, two things she'd been missing for the past three days. The weather had been cold and miserable but still no snow, and she hadn't seen or heard from Rick since they'd left Victor's house on Thursday and went off in different directions. Rick to go back to work, and Jodi to go to Finch Realty in hopes of catching Farley in so they could reprice her property for sale now that there was no longer a house on it.

Unfortunately, when she'd gotten there, she was told that he was out of town and wouldn't be back in the office until Monday, which left her at loose ends until after the week-end.

She sat up in bed and hugged her bent legs to her chest. At the time she'd been delighted, expecting Rick to take up her spare time. After that torrid kiss at the Stuarts' she was sure their relationship was heating up, going some-where, but although she'd stayed close to the house and the telephone he neither came over nor called.

She sighed and buried her face in her knees. What had

gone wrong? That was a question she'd agonized over during the long, dark, boring days, and the sleepless nights.

In reviewing the events of that afternoon she realized that he'd been quieter, almost withdrawn, after she and Victor came downstairs with the twins. She'd been so euphoric from the kiss and so engrossed in the adorable little girls that she hadn't noticed Rick's change of mood at the time. He hadn't acted angry or put out because the babies had stolen the spotlight, but on looking back he'd seemed disinterested, almost sad.

She raised her head and stared vacantly across the room. Could it have been the youngsters? Was he really that disinterested in children? He'd made it plain to her that he didn't intend to have any of his own, but she got the impression that he was concerned about overpopulation and the violence in the world today rather than having an actual aversion to them.

Well, she wasn't going to mope around the house any longer. Neither was she going to throw herself at him and hope she could change his mind.

Tossing off the covers, she got out of bed and put on her robe, then headed for the bathroom. She had an appointment to see Farley Finch at ten-thirty, and she was going to tell him to price the lot for a quick sale and send her check to her address in Cincinnati when it was sold. She'd had enough of Richard McBride's on-again off-again idea of romance.

She was going home!

Jodi was ushered into Farley's office that morning as soon as she arrived. He looked rather pale, and he didn't rise from his chair behind the desk as he usually did when she entered the room, but he smiled and motioned for her to sit down across from him.

"I heard about the fire," he said consolingly. "God but

I'm sorry, Jodi. I understand it was arson. Do they have any leads on who did it?"

She sat down. "Not that I know of," she said, deliberately not mentioning that she'd been their first suspect. Everybody in town probably knew it by now, but she wasn't going to be a party to spreading the story around.

"The house was insured," she continued, "but I might have trouble trying to collect on it until we find out exactly what happened and why. Will that hold up the sale of the lot?"

Farley rubbed his chin. "I shouldn't think so. The house is no longer part of the property. The burned-out hulk will have to be cleared away, and, of course, we'll have to come down on the price considerably."

"Yes, I understand that," she told him. "It doesn't matter. I just want to put it on the market and then go back home to Cincinnati. You won't need me here, will you?"

He looked startled, but masked it quickly. "No, not at all. I can send you the papers to sign. Be leaving soon, will you?"

"Within a couple of days, I hope," she answered. "Can you give me some idea of what the lot alone is worth?"

"I can't tell you until I've taken a look at it," he said. "I don't know how much damage was done."

Jodi hoped that reevaluating the place wasn't going to be a long, drawn-out process. "The house is a complete loss. It's just a pile of rubble, and all of the bushes and vines next to it were burned, but Shawn says it looks like most of the trees can be saved."

"I'm going over there now," Farley told her. "You're welcome to come with me if you'd like. We can probably get the new contract drawn up and signed today if we can agree on a price."

That last sentence brought a sinking feeling to Jodi's stomach. That was what she'd thought she wanted to hear, but now that it was a possibility she felt sick instead of relieved. Talking about leaving Copper Canyon was easy, but now that all the obstacles had been cleared away, she was going to be expected to follow through and do it.

The prospect shouldn't be so painful. It was past time for her to get away from here. If this was love she felt for Rick, then it was highly overrated. Love should make a person happy, not sad. Hopeful, not depressed. Trusting, not doubtful.

"Jodi?" Farley prompted, interrupting her brooding.

"Oh! Yes, thank you, I'd like to go with you."

He smiled but then winced as he stood, moving more slowly than usual. He seemed to be favoring his right side, and she wondered if he was bothered with muscle spasms or arthritis.

"Why don't you ride in my car with me?" he offered. "We'll no doubt have to come back here afterward, anyway."

She stood, too. "Thank you, I will," she agreed, and as she followed him out of the room she noticed that he was wearing an oversized sweatshirt with his slacks instead of one of the sport jackets he always wore. Usually he didn't dress that casually for the office.

Farley and Jodi poked around the lot for nearly an hour, and when they got back to his office he did some figuring on his calculator and quoted a price. It was lower than she'd expected, and she named a higher one.

"Jodi, you're being unrealistic," he said in exasperation. "Surely you've noticed that the area out there is not a desirable one."

He picked up the small calculator and did some more figuring, then looked at her. "Tell you what I'll do. I'll buy the land myself, as is, at my estimate, and I'll pay to have it cleaned off. That way you can go on home with all the business of your aunt's estate settled, and I can take my time reselling it and try to make at least some profit."

She was too tired and depressed to argue anymore. All she wanted was to have it settled.

"All right," she said despondently. "Have the contract drawn up and I'll sign it."

Jodi didn't get back to the McBrides' house until early afternoon. Shawn and Dorothy were just finishing lunch, but Dorothy had saved a plate in the oven for her. She had to bite her lip to keep from sobbing. She was going to miss these two wonderful people. Almost as much as she was going to miss their maddening son, but she didn't dare think about that.

While she ate she told them about her meeting with Farley. They were both surprised and dismayed, and wondered aloud if she was doing the right thing.

"It's not worth fussing over," she told them, "and I really do have to get back to Cincinnati. I have a job there that I enjoy very much and don't want to lose. I...I expect to leave the day after tomorrow."

Dorothy put her hand over Jodi's where it lay on the table. "We're just being selfish, my dear. We'll miss you."

This time Jodi couldn't hold back the sob. "I'll miss you, too. I wish I could take you both home with me."

"And we wish we could keep you here with us," Dorothy countered. "Does Rick know yet that you're leaving?"

Sadly she shook her head. "No, but it won't matter to him."

Shawn spoke up. "I think it will matter very much to him," he murmured.

Jodi didn't comment, just thanked them, then excused herself to go upstairs and take a nap. She hadn't slept well for the past three nights. Every time she closed her eyes she relived that kiss and all the erotic sensations it had aroused in her, only now they tormented rather than pleasured. Would she ever experience that exhilaration with any other man?

Slipping out of her shoes, slacks and blouse, she wrapped herself in her warm robe and climbed into bed.

Jodi woke two hours later feeling rested and better able to face the fact that she had to gather up her clothes and start packing. It would be difficult to leave, but maybe the long drive home would focus her mind on the happiness of getting back to her work and her friends rather than on the anguish of leaving Rick and his parents behind.

She dressed in jeans and a gray sweatshirt, then rounded up items that needed to be washed and took them to the laundry room in the basement. As she wandered through the house she noticed that she was alone. Apparently Shawn and Dorothy had gone off somewhere.

She'd just put her laundry in the washing machine and turned it on when she heard the phone ringing upstairs. After hurrying up the steps, she grabbed the nearest phone, the one in the kitchen. "Hello," she said breathlessly.

There was a pause at the other end of the line, then a man's voice said, "Jodi, this is Rick."

Immediately her traitorous heart speeded up, and once more, in her dreams, she was in his arms.

With a jolt of disgust at herself she blanked out her video-screen mind and took a deep breath. "Yes, Rick?"

He cleared his throat. "How are you?"

How do you think I am, dammit? Her pain formed the words, but her pride stopped them before they could tumble out. "Fine, thank you," she said stiffly. "And you?"

Why didn't he get to the point! Was he playing games with her? After all, he'd deliberately kissed her with smoldering passion and then acted as if it never happened. Was he the type who enticed women just to see how far they'd go?

No, she couldn't believe he'd be that despicable!

"I...I'm fine, too," he said after a slight pause.

Obviously this conversation wasn't going anywhere, and she was just about to ring off when he spoke again. "Jodi, can I speak to my mother, please?"

She flinched as if from a blow. So that was it. He'd called to talk to Dorothy and got her instead, then floundered and didn't know what to say. She'd been a fool to think he'd wanted to speak with her.

She swallowed and prayed that her voice would be steady. "I'm sorry, Rick," she said coolly. "Neither Shawn nor Dorothy are here. I don't know where they are. I just woke up from a nap and they were gone. Did you want to leave a message?"

"Aren't you feeling well?" he asked anxiously, as if it mattered to him one way or the other.

"I feel fine," she snapped. "Do you want me to ask Dorothy to call you when she comes in?"

There was silence for a moment, then he said, "No, I..." Another pause, then, "Uh, Jodi, would you mind doing me a favor? I wouldn't ask you if I weren't in a real bind," he hurried to assure her, "but I'm expecting a big heavy combination refrigerator-freezer to be delivered to my house sometime between now and six o'clock and they won't leave it unless there's someone there to accept it. Even if they would I couldn't wrestle it into the kitchen by myself, but I can't get away from the station for that long. I was going to ask Mother to go over and wait for it. Is there any chance you could do that for me? It's really important."

Jodi sighed. The only thing he needed her for was to let the men in to deliver a refrigerator. Well, she couldn't very well refuse. She owed him big time for fixing it with his parents to let her stay with them for three weeks.

"Yes, of course I will," she said. "It's no trouble, but I don't have a key to your house."

"Oh, damn, that's right." He sounded frustrated. "And

Mom probably has hers with her on her key ring. Look, if you could leave right now, I'll have Evelyn meet you at my house with my key. She should get there about the same time you do. I really appreciate this, Jodi. I can't tell you how much."

She didn't want his gratitude, or his shame for leading her on, then dropping her. All she wanted was his love, and it was abundantly clear that she'd never get that.

"It's no more than I owe you, Rick," she said crisply. "I'm leaving right now."

She hung up the phone before he could reply.

Jodi turned into Rick's driveway just moments before his dispatcher-secretary pulled up to the curb. They both got out of their cars and met at the porch. Evelyn handed Jodi the key, and Jodi thanked her and invited her to come in, but she declined, explaining that she had to get back to work.

Jodi thanked her again, climbed the two steps to the covered cement porch and let herself in the house. She hadn't been there since Rick brought her over to shower and change out of her wet clothes on the rainy day when she arrived in Copper Canyon.

She walked through the small entry to the living room which was at the back of the house. The afternoon light streamed through the large sliding glass doors that lead to the redwood deck. It looked warm, but even with her parka on she realized it was chilly inside. She searched the walls for the heating thermostat until she found it and turned it up a few degrees.

Built-in bookshelves took up part of one wall, and contained an assortment of trophies and bric-a-brac as well as paperback novels and hardcover textbooks on police procedure. She'd forgotten to bring something to read while she waited, but, unfortunately, the novels were all westerns and adventure with a few of the more violent detective stories mixed in. None of which interested her.

The wood and leather furnishings and earth-colored walls were as masculine and comfortable as she'd remembered, and there was a place for everything and everything in its place. Rick was a meticulous housekeeper. There were no clothes on the floor, dirty dishes in the sink or papers and magazines scattered in disarray on the tables.

He took pride in his home and kept it neat and clean. A man after her own heart, except he didn't have to go after that, it was already his if he'd just accept it.

She took off her parka and tossed it across one of the chairs, then turned on the big screen television. About all that was on were reruns of old series on local area stations or continuous news on cable. She decided on the news and settled down in Rick's comfortable recliner to wait for the delivery truck.

After forty minutes of watching more or less the same news repeated every fifteen minutes, Jodi became restless and stood. She walked into the kitchen, which was at the front of the house, and noticed that the old refrigerator still stood where it had been the last time she was here, but it had been unplugged and cleaned out. That meant the delivery men would have to take it out to put the new one in. She hoped Rick had given them instructions on where he wanted the old one placed or disposed of because she had no idea.

A glance out the window over the sink revealed a quiet street with no delivery trucks in sight, and she sighed. She hated sitting around with nothing to do.

The loud ring of the telephone shattered the silence and startled her. Her first inclination was to let it ring. After all, she didn't live here, so it wasn't likely to be for her.

On second thought, it might be Rick. Maybe he wanted to give her more instructions for the delivery people. The problem was she didn't know where to find the phone. She could see that it wasn't in the kitchen, but the sound seemed to be coming from the area across the entry hall, where the bedrooms and bath were.

Quickly she followed the ring and found the instrument in Rick's bedroom. Snatching it up she said, "Hello."

Nobody answered, but she could hear someone breathing. She tried again, louder. "Hello!"

Still no answer.

This type of thing always annoyed her. Usually she just hung up, but maybe the party on the other end was surprised to hear a woman's voice answering and thought they had the wrong number.

She tried one last time. "This is the residence of Chief of Police Richard McBride. He's not here at the moment, but I'll take a message if you'd like to leave one."

A woman's voice finally spoke hesitantly. "Will someone be there at the house for the next hour or so?"

Jodi relaxed and spoke more politely. "Oh, you must be calling about the delivery of the refrigerator-freezer."

A slight pause, then, "Yes..." She cleared her throat and started again, still sounding nervous. "Yes, I am. Will you or Mr. McBride be there?"

"Yes, I will," Jodi confirmed. "I'm expecting you."

"Good," the woman answered and hung up before Jodi could ask for a more exact time of arrival.

That's odd, Jodi thought as she returned the phone to its cradle. Usually spokespersons for businesses were trained to modulate their voices so that they sounded loud, clear and, above all, friendly. This woman sounded uncertain and almost...afraid?

Oh, well, business practices were probably different in small towns. She left the bedroom and went back to the living room, where she once more turned on the television and sat down with the remote control to skim the menu.

Choosing a rerun of an episode from the classic series "The Rockford Files," she curled up in the chair and soon became engrossed in trying to follow the plot steps and keep the characters straight.

So much so that she jumped when the doorbell rang. Good heavens, they were here with the refrigerator and she hadn't even heard the truck drive up! She scrambled out of the chair and rushed to the door where she unlocked it and flung it open.

There was no one there! She pushed open the screen and turned her head to look up and down the street, but there was no truck, either!

Well, for heaven's sake, where were they? Someone had rung the bell, and it wasn't the telephone, either. It had a different sound altogether.

Puzzled, she lowered her gaze, and that's when she saw it: a medium-size wicker carrying basket with a high bent handle across the middle sitting on the porch on the other side of the open screen door where it wasn't readily visible.

She stepped outside, then pushed the door shut and stared. There was something in the receptacle. It looked like torn-up bedding.

Hunkering down beside it she saw the basket was old and worn with broken reeds here and there. Cautiously she reached out and touched the top of the soiled contents. It was a ragged piece of lightweight blanket. Was this someone's idea of a joke? Or maybe a litter of newborn kittens somebody wanted to get rid of?

Her hand trembled as she pulled the blanket aside, then she gasped and put her fist to her mouth to stifle a shriek of shock and amazement at what she saw.

It was a baby! Surely no more than a few days old, tucked into the basket on a makeshift bed and sound asleep with its tiny thumb in its mouth!

Chapter Nine

A chilling breeze blew across the porch and snapped Jodi out of her stupor with the reminder that it was cold out there, and the pile of rags surrounding the infant were thin and inadequate.

Carefully she picked the basket up by the handle and took it into the house, where she carried it into the kitchen and set it on the counter at one side of the sink. Her hands were cold, and she turned on the hot water and held them under it until they were warm, then felt for the pulse at the side of the child's neck. She found a strong steady beat and the skin felt tepid to the touch, which she hoped meant the sleep was natural and not fever-induced.

Thank God, the poor little thing appeared to be healthy. She didn't want to wake it up if she could help it. Gently she grasped the piece of blanket it was wrapped in and opened it all the way. The baby was awfully small, but looked to be full-term, or nearly so. It was dressed in a faded flowered kimono with nothing underneath but a disposable diaper. Jodi unfastened the Velcro on one side and determined that the diaper was wet and the remnant of the umbilical cord was still attached, but it was tied awkwardly with an old piece of string. The infant was a girl.

Jodi rewrapped her in the blanket, then searched the basket by running her hand along the inside between the bedding and the reeds. There was nothing there, no note or any indication of who she belonged to or why she'd been left on Rick's porch. There wasn't even a spare diaper.

Jodi was still stunned with shock, but the one thing she knew for sure was that she had to notify Rick and then get the baby to a doctor. It looked to her as if the child had been born without medical assistance, and that umbilical cord could easily be infected. Also, when this little girl woke up she was going to be hungry, and Jodi didn't even have a bottle, let alone formula.

Grasping the basket by the handle once more, she carried it with her into Rick's bedroom where the telephone was and set it on the bed beside her as she picked up the phone and dialed O.

The operator put her through to Rick at the police station, but when he answered, her mind went blank. How was she going to tell him what had happened without making him think she'd lost her mind completely? She was almost certain that the good people of Copper Canyon didn't go around every day leaving newborn babies on doorsteps!

"Hello," he said again, louder and more commanding than the first. "Who is this? Do you have an emergency? Talk to me!"

She finally collected her wits about her enough to speak. "Rick, this is Jodi."

"Jodi?" He sounded puzzled. "Is something the matter?"

"Yes! Please come home. I need you."

"Sweetheart, are you all right?" Even in her panic she didn't miss the endearment, or the urgency that vibrated in his tone.

"No. I mean yes, I'm okay, but we need to go to the doctor."

She knew she wasn't making sense, but she couldn't think coherently.

"I'll be right there," Rick said and hung up.

Good. Rick will be here soon. He'll know what to do.

She took the basket into the living room. It was like transporting a doll around the house. In fact, it was alarmingly like transporting a doll. Surely a real live baby should have wakened by now. She'd not only been carrying it around but she'd unwrapped and examined it, and she'd made no attempt to keep her voice down when she was talking on the phone to Rick.

Also, how had the child gotten on the porch? Someone had to have brought it here, but she hadn't heard anything or anyone until the doorbell rang. She'd answered the door immediately, but no one was in sight and there were no cars in the street.

The sound of tires skidding on pavement alerted her that Rick was here. She stood, but before she could take a step the doorbell rang, one long insistent ring, and she remembered that she had his key.

Immediately the infant twitched and started to howl as Rick pounded on the door and called her name. She ran to let him in.

He caught her in his arms and gasped, "Jodi, for the love of God, what's wrong?"

Before she could answer he raised his head. "What's that?" he barked, then stared at her. "Have you got a baby here?"

She pulled away from him and caught his hand. "Come and see," she said and sprinted with him to the living room.

Rick stared in openmouthed amazement at the basket on the sofa and its contents. "Holy sh—shucks!" he finished delicately. "Where did you get that?"

She leaned down and picked up the wailing baby and

held it in her arms. It weighed hardly anything, but there was surely nothing wrong with her lungs.

"You woke her up," she accused.

"Her?" he managed to choke out.

"Yes, it's a little girl," Jodi told him, "and her diaper's wet, but I don't have another one. Also, she's no doubt hungry, and I need formula."

Again she knew she was being inarticulate, but her thoughts kept running ahead of her tongue.

Rick put his hands on her shoulders and looked directly at her. "Jodi, please, take a deep breath and start at the beginning," he said tenderly. "Where did this baby come from?"

"The porch," she said anxiously. "I'll tell you all about it, but right now we have to take her to a doctor. She seems to be healthy, but—"

"We'll take her to the doctor," he assured her, "but first I have to know where you got her. How long have you had her?"

Even in Jodi's agitated state she knew he was right, and she tried to think straight and answer his questions. "Someone rang the doorbell just a few minutes ago. I thought it was the delivery men, but when I went to let them in there was nobody there. Instead, the basket was sitting on the porch with the baby in it. I brought it in, examined her and then called you."

Rick listened in silent bewilderment. Someone left a baby on his doorstep? But that was ridiculous! He was a bachelor and lived alone. He'd also let it be known that he didn't want children, so why would anyone give him their unwanted infant?

He looked down at the wailing little creature in Jodi's arms. Its face was red with exertion, its eyes screwed up and its tiny fists flailing at the world.

His heart turned over. How could anyone abandon such a tiny helpless little bundle? With all the people who wanted children and couldn't have them, there was no excuse for just throwing one away, like a broken doll!

Still, Jodi was right. They had to set the wheels in motion to get this little one taken care of, and the first step was Dr. Sam. Jodi could fill in the missing blanks for Rick later.

He called the doctor's office and explained that he had an emergency patient whom they were bringing in, then bundled Jodi and the baby, whom she'd wrapped in a thick warm towel over the lightweight blanket, into his police car. The child still cried but not quite as noisily.

At his office, Dr. Sam Lawford examined the baby while Jodi told him how she and Rick had come by it. She'd found the doctor to be a good-looking man in his late thirties with brown curly hair and brown eyes that were flecked with green. There was a warm, caring tone to his voice, and his smile was guaranteed to melt resistance.

The child had taken to him immediately when he took her in his arms and put a pacifier in her mouth. For now she seemed to be content to suck on that, at least until she found out, as she would soon, that there was no nourishment in it.

"Are you telling me that someone put this child on Rick's porch and disappeared?" Dr. Sam asked incredulously.

"That's right," she insisted. "I couldn't believe it, either. What if I hadn't been there? Rick was at work, and—"

She stopped in midsentence as her own words brought back another conversation.

Both men looked at her and she blinked. "I forgot," she said thoughtfully. "There was a phone call about half an hour before the doorbell rang. It was a woman asking for Rick— No, wait, when I picked it up nobody answered at first. I thought it was one of Rick's girlfriends who wasn't expecting a woman to answer the phone—"

"What girlfriend?" Rick interrupted. "I'm not seeing anybody."

Jodi was delighted to hear that, but she apologized, anyway. "I'm sorry. I didn't mean to infer that you were, but I told her that whoever was calling had reached your number and although you weren't there I'd relay a message if she wanted to leave one."

Again she turned her attention to Dr. Sam. "That's when the woman spoke. She asked if anyone would be at the house for the next hour or so. I thought she was from the delivery crew. In fact, I asked if she was and she said yes, but then she hung up quite abruptly."

Jodi looked from the doctor to Rick. "Could it have been the mother calling to make sure someone would be there to find the child?"

"That's very probable," Rick said, "but I'll also check with the delivery people and see if anyone there made a call. Can you tell me how she sounded?"

Jodi shrugged. "She sounded hesitant, which I thought was a little odd since business people are usually self-confident, but other than that there was nothing distinctive."

Dr. Sam put the baby on the examining table and undressed her. "That umbilical cord needs attention," he murmured as his hand roamed over the tiny body, "but there are no respiratory problems. She's been cleaned up, but God only knows when or how. Probably in a rest room somewhere."

Jodi winced. How utterly awful! For both the child and the mother.

Apparently Rick noticed because he put his arm around her shoulders. "She'll be all right, honey," he said soothingly. "We'll see to it that she's taken care of. The mother must still be around here close."

That jolted Jodi. "You're not going to give the child

back to *her,* are you? I mean, she obviously can't take care of the baby or she wouldn't have abandoned her!''

''Don't worry,'' he said. ''The Child Protective Agency will make sure she has a good home.''

Rick squeezed her, then released her as Dr. Sam picked the infant up and put it on the scale. ''Mmm,'' he muttered. ''Weight's five pounds on the dot. As a precaution we'll put her in the hospital for a few days until that goes up a little, but I wouldn't call her premature. Not more than a week or so, anyway. I'd guess she's less than twenty-four hours old.''

Rick nodded. ''Okay, we'll take her over to the hospital, and then I'll call child welfare and tell them to start looking for a place for her.''

Jodi didn't like the sound of that. ''What do you mean, 'looking for a place for her'?''

''I mean a foster home,'' he explained. ''We only have a couple of those in the community, and most of the time it's not enough. We may have to leave this youngster in the hospital for a while until we can find foster parents who have room for her.''

''No!'' Jodi protested. ''Let me have her.'' Once the words were out of her mouth, they surprised her as much as they did the men. What was she thinking of? She'd already made plans to go back to Cincinnati in the next day or two. She had a job to get back to!

On the other hand she didn't need the salary, and she couldn't bear to think of this poor little abandoned baby being turned over to an already overworked foster mother. Jodi could devote full-time to the child, and she was well-trained.

''What?'' the men said in unison, and again the baby started to cry. Dr. Sam took her off the scales and laid her on the table again, then started putting a fresh disposable diaper on her.

''I mean... Well, that is...let me take care of her until

you can find a foster family. I'm well qualified. I have a degree in early childhood education and have been working as a preschool teacher and caregiver. I'm at least as knowledgeable as a foster mother, and I wouldn't even charge for it."

"But you don't have any equipment or clothes for an infant," Rick reminded her, "and *where* are you planning to take care of her? At Dad and Mom's house? I think you should discuss that with them before you go making any rash promises."

Jodi cringed. He was right. She couldn't impose a newborn baby on his parents. They'd no doubt had all the screaming kids, midnight feedings and dirty diapers they could stomach over the years.

"No, I..." She hesitated. So what *was* she proposing?

Suddenly a thought occurred to her. "I can rent an apartment or a small house," she said triumphantly.

Rick shook his head. "Honey," he said quietly. "You're talking nonsense. You don't even live here in Copper Canyon. What about your home and your job in Cincinnati? Your parents in Atlanta? Besides, this child's mother could come forward at any time and claim her."

"But you said—"

"I said we'd find a good home for her, and we will, but that doesn't preclude the mother. She still has first claim if she's able to prove that she can and will take care of her daughter."

Jodi knew this, but she didn't want to face it. She couldn't stand the thought of giving the baby back to the woman who had so callously abandoned her. What if she did it again, and the infant wasn't found quickly enough to prevent a disaster?

Realizing that she wasn't altogether thinking clearly, Jodi decided not to argue with Rick about it now. They'd take the little doll over to the hospital, where she'd be checked more thoroughly and sheltered until morning.

Meanwhile Jodi would have time to calm down and straighten out her thinking, tell Rick's parents what had happened and discuss it with them and muster up arguments that were solid and well thought out enough for Rick to take them seriously before bringing in the child welfare people.

"Will you at least hold off reporting the baby as an abandoned child until tomorrow?" she pleaded.

He looked sympathetic but uncertain. "Jodi, I'm required by law to report it."

She hated taking advantage of their friendship and his natural generosity, but felt too strongly about this to give up. "I know, but surely a few hours won't make any difference. She'll have to stay in the hospital at least overnight anyway, and she'll get the best possible care there. Please, Rick. Give me a chance to work something out!"

His gaze searched her face, and she neither blinked nor looked away.

Finally he sighed and broke contact. "All right," he said reluctantly. "If it means so much to you, and if Sam goes along with it, I'll wait until tomorrow, but that's all."

She wanted to throw her arms around him, hug him and show her appreciation with kisses, but in the past few days he'd made it plain that he didn't want that sort of familiarity from her. Instead, she smiled wistfully and touched his cheek with her fingers.

"Thank you." It came out as little more than a whisper.

His eyes darkened with what looked a lot like pain as he reached up, took her hand and kissed her palm. "Tomorrow, Jodi. No later," he said and released her hand.

It was well past dark by the time Rick and Jodi left the hospital after registering the baby in and seeing her settled comfortably in a private room. They couldn't put her in the maternity nursery because she hadn't been born in the hospital but had come from outside and was not considered sterile.

As they got in his car Rick said, "Is your car at my house or did you walk over from Dad and Mom's?"

She settled herself in the seat as he started the engine. "It's sitting in the driveway at your house," she told him. "I guess you didn't notice when you drove up earlier."

"Hell, you had me so scared that I couldn't think of anything except that something awful must have happened to upset you so!" he grated. "I was afraid you were in mortal danger. The last thing I expected was to find you with an abandoned baby."

"I'm sorry I frightened you, but I was in a state of shock." She smiled to herself. "I mean, when I opened that blanket and found a newborn baby..."

"I know the feeling exactly," he confessed.

A few seconds later they drove up in front of Rick's house. "Would you like to come in for a drink, or a cup of coffee? I have a supply of frozen dinners in the freezer—"

He stopped abruptly and groaned. "Oh damn, I forgot about the refrigerator."

"So did I," Jodi admitted regretfully. "Will the store reschedule delivery?"

He turned off the engine. "Yeah, but I'll probably have to wait a while."

They got out of the car, and he came around to take her arm. "Rick," she said, "why don't you come over to your folks' house with me? They have a whole refrigerator and freezer full of food. I'm sure they won't mind if we fix ourselves something to eat, and," she said, with a teasing chuckle, "you can tell them all about your new baby."

"*My* new baby!" he said in mock horror. "Bite your

tongue, young lady. We'll tell them about *your* new baby.''

A feeling of warmth flooded over Jodi. Was that a slip of the tongue that meant he was inclined to help her get temporary custody of the child until permanent arrangements could be made? Oh, she hoped so!

She laughed and squeezed his arm. ''That's fine with me, but first I have to go into your house for a minute. I forgot my purse when I left, and it has my car keys in it.''

They walked toward the house, and when they got there Rick unlocked the door and turned on the lights. ''Do you mind waiting a few minutes until I plug in the old refrigerator, check my answering machine and call the station to make sure everything is running smoothly there?''

''Not at all,'' she assured him. ''I'll wait in the parlor.''

He turned into the kitchen and she walked ahead to the living room. The first thing she saw was the beat-up old basket sitting on the sofa. She'd taken the child out of it and carried her to the hospital, but now it seemed to draw her.

Where had the basket come from? Probably someone's trash pile. It looked old and worn.

She sat down beside it and touched it. The poor little baby. How pitiful to be welcomed into the world with nothing but a junked carrier and a heap of rags.

Where had the rags come from? Now that the top one that had been used to wrap the infant in was gone she could see that the padding was part of the same torn-up thin cotton blanket.

Picking it up she gave it a shake, and to her surprise a piece of paper fell out and onto her lap.

Gingerly she picked it up. It was a sheet of lined tablet paper folded twice into a rectangle.

Her heart pounded. Was this the note she'd looked for and failed to find earlier? The information on the baby and why the mother had given it away? It had apparently been between a couple of the folds in the padding.

Without a second thought she opened it. There were only a few lines, written large and in pencil. It read:

Rick, darling, I wasn't cut out to be a mother, but I know you'll be a great father. Take good care of our little girl.

There was no signature.

Chapter Ten

Jodi stared at the words written on the paper as they turned into a foreign language and ran together into a blur, making her head whirl and her ears roar.

Instinctively she bent over and put her forehead on her knees until the noise stopped. When she straightened she found that the dizziness and blur were gone.

She gazed down at the paper, which was now crumbled in her fist. Unwittingly she opened her hand and let it drop to her lap, then picked it up and smoothed it out to read again. It still said the same thing:

Rick, darling, I wasn't cut out to be a mother, but I know you'll be a great father. Take good care of our little girl.

No signature, no address, no birthdate, no instructions.

Had Rick gotten a girl pregnant and then deserted her?

A wave of disbelief washed over Jodi. That was unthinkable! Rick wouldn't do such a thing. He was too kind, too responsible, too good a man, to do that.

But the baby was all too real. It couldn't be explained away. And why would the mother leave her daughter on Rick's doorstep and name him as the father if he wasn't?

She was still sitting there, shaken to the core, when Rick wandered in. "Okay, I'm ready to go," he announced, then stopped and looked at her.

"Jodi?" he said tentatively, then more urgently, "Jodi, what's the matter? You're white as a ghost!"

She heard him as from a distance, and couldn't bring herself to raise her head and look up as he hurried toward her.

"Honey, what's happened?" He hunkered down in front of her and took her chin in his hand to turn her head toward him. "Jodi, talk to me. Are you sick?"

Her gaze met his, and she saw the anxiety in his expression, but still she couldn't speak. Instead, she held out the paper.

"What's this?" he asked as he took it. She noticed that she'd crumpled it again, and he had to smooth it out to read it.

"What in hell!" he thundered and jumped up. "Son of a— Where did you get this?"

He glowered down at her, and his rage somehow shook her out of her stupor. It was replaced by a building anger. "It was in the bottom of the basket," she said tartly as she also stood. "Rick, how could you?"

"How could I what?" he bellowed. "Surely you don't believe this garbage!"

"How can I not?" she asked, tight-lipped. "The baby's mother would certainly know who the father was."

"Well, obviously this mother didn't, because it sure as hell wasn't me."

The more he denied parentage, the madder she got. "What did you do, just write her off when she told you she was pregnant?"

His face turned red. "I've never gotten a woman pregnant, and I'm not going to be held accountable for some other man's slipup."

"I can't believe you'd refuse to take responsibility for your own daughter," she taunted. "I know you don't want children, but the least you could do is acknowledge paternity and pay child support."

He ran his fingers through his hair. "Dammit, Jodi, if the infant was mine I'd gladly raise and support her, but she's not mine, and no woman is going to railroad me into thinking she is."

Jodi caught the word *gladly* and it somehow didn't fit but she was too upset to figure out why.

She took a deep breath. "All right," she said, making an effort to speak calmly. "Even if, as you claim, you didn't know your girlfriend was pregnant, how can you be so sure her baby isn't yours?"

"Because, in the first place I don't have a 'girlfriend,' and in the second place I take steps to make sure any woman I'm intimate with won't conceive. It's called birth control, in case you haven't heard," he concluded sarcastically.

"I've heard," she snapped. "But I also know that even the most reliable contraceptives are not totally foolproof."

He nodded his head in her direction. "Thank you, Dr. Ruth, but I was already aware of that and still I know for a fact that I'm not this child's father."

"Oh?" she asked derisively. "And how can you be so sure?"

He jammed his hands in his pockets and slumped tiredly. "Easily," he said. "It just takes a rudimentary knowledge of mathematics. According to my calendar this is early November, right?"

Jodi was puzzled but nodded her agreement. "And it takes nine months gestation to bring a fetus to full-term. Right again?"

She was beginning to see what he was getting at. "Yes," she agreed haltingly.

"That means the infant was conceived in early February, and I didn't have sex with any woman during that time."

Startled, Jodi blinked. "Are you sure?"

He uttered a short, derisive chuckle. "Who would know better than me? Certainly not you. You didn't even know I existed then."

She had to admit that he had a point. "But the baby was small. Even the doctor said she could have been a week or two early."

Rick sighed. "It wouldn't have mattered. Dammit, Jodi, what kind of bastard do you think I am? I don't make love with every woman I date, and I don't have one-night stands."

She had no answer for that, and she had to admit that his version of his behavior was much more in sync with the way he'd treated her since she'd known him than her accusation of him was. But why would any woman name him as the father of her child if he wasn't?

On the other hand, what kind of mother would abandon her baby on a stranger's porch?

Wearily she sank back down on the couch. Her head whirled and her mind seemed to have stopped functioning altogether. Was it possible that he was telling her the truth? If he was, she was doing him a great disservice by not believing him, but if he was lying, then he deserved everything she was dishing out.

"What are you going to tell your parents?" she asked anxiously.

"The truth, of course," he answered simply. "Obviously someone is either trying to blacken my name or is determined to make me responsible for a child I didn't father. All I can do is ride it out and hope that my fellow townspeople have more faith in my sense of honor than you do."

He spoke softly, but that last sentence hit her like a blow, and she clenched her jaws to keep from crying out with the pain. Was she wrongfully accusing him?

Rick didn't seem to notice. "I'd better get over to the house and tell Mom and Dad before they hear it from someone else," he continued. "Word gets around fast in a small town."

He turned and walked toward the door, and a few seconds later she heard it open, then close behind him.

Jodi leaned back against the sofa. She felt drained and exhausted. Had she been wrong to take that letter at face value and attack Rick so viciously? It was totally unlike him to deny parentage of his own child.

Or was it? She'd known him only three weeks, and a good share of that time they'd spent apart. He'd been open and aboveboard with her about not wanting children when he could have gone ahead and seduced her. She wouldn't have known about that complication until it was too late to keep from falling hopelessly in love with him.

Unfortunately, she'd done that anyway, but at least he'd warned her they had no future together. Was it so difficult to believe he'd be as honest with any woman he was attracted to?

But accidental pregnancies could and did happen. Jodi had no way of knowing how he'd act if faced with something like that.

Still, it was plain to see that she'd hurt him badly by doubting him. Didn't that indicate he was telling the truth?

With a sigh she pushed herself forward and stood. All this introspection was only getting her more muddled and giving her a headache besides. All she could do now was go to his parents' home and hope that once he'd told them the situation they could make some sense of it and explain it to her.

A few minutes later Jodi pulled her car up to the curb in front of the McBride residence. Rick's auto was parked in the driveway.

Although she had a key, she knocked on the door and waited, unable to bring herself to just walk in as she usually did. This time she couldn't be sure if she'd be welcome or not. She felt like a traitor, but she still had doubts.

Rick opened the door. "Come in, Jodi." His tone was impersonal. "I've just finished telling Mom and Dad what happened. You can join us if you'd like."

He sounded as if it didn't matter to him one way or the other what she did.

"Not unless you want me to," she said as she stepped inside.

He closed the door behind her and shrugged. "It's your decision."

He really was upset with her, and she knew the proper thing for her to do was to go upstairs to her room and give the family some privacy for their discussion.

She also knew she wasn't going to. "In that case I'd like to join you," she said and walked with him into the living room.

Dorothy and Shawn were both flabbergasted and thoroughly upset. "Rick says you found the baby on the porch," Dorothy said. "How could any woman abandon her child like that? And then try to make Rick believe he's the father!"

Obviously Rick had told his parents the entire story, even though he probably could have concealed the letter and its implication. After all, she and he were the only ones who knew about that.

He probably didn't trust *her* not to tell them, Jodi thought sadly, but she would never have done that.

As they discussed the incident, she realized that once Rick had told his parents the child wasn't his it never even occurred to them to doubt his word. Also it was obvious he hadn't told them that she did doubt it. They just assumed she was as sure of his innocence as they were.

Oh, God, if only she were.

Later, over supper, the question came up as to what would happen to the child now, and Jodi reiterated her desire to take care of it until a permanent home could be found.

"I'd like to rent an apartment temporarily if the authorities will let me have her," she concluded.

Rick frowned, but Dorothy beamed. "What a marvelous idea," she said happily, "but there's no need to rent an apartment. We have plenty of space here. We can use Jessica's room for a nursery. It's all furnished. All we'll have to do is take out one of the twin beds and install a crib—"

"Now wait just a minute, dammit," Rick broke in angrily. "Mom, that kid is not your grandchild, and you have no obligation toward her. She's just an abandoned baby like millions of others, and the child welfare agencies will see that she's taken care of. That's their job."

Dorothy blinked in astonishment. "Of course she's not my grandchild. You said it wasn't your baby and I have no reason to doubt you, but she needs a temporary home. Jodi has the energy, and your father and I have the room, to take care of her. I don't see how you can possibly object."

He slumped in defeat. "Have you thought of how this is going to look? People will say that you've taken her in and are caring for her because I'm her father and refuse to acknowledge her. Is that the kind of rumor you want going around?"

A little of the glow went out of his mother, but determination flashed from her eyes. "Frankly, son, I don't give a tinker's damn what people say. They'll find something else to talk about in a month or so, but if it will make you uncomfortable, then your dad and I won't get involved."

Her gaze switched to Jodi. "However, I can't speak for Jodi..."

"Everyone knows I've been here only a few weeks so there will be no reason for the townspeople to think I'd have a personal interest in taking care of Rick's baby," she reasoned. "I can just rent an apartment and act as a foster mother to the child."

She turned to glance at him. He looked exhausted, bewildered and resentful, all perfectly understandable. He'd really had a rough day and no doubt there were a lot more of them in store for him before this mess was cleared up. She hated to add to his burdens, but this was important to her regardless of whose baby it was.

"Please, Rick," she said pleadingly. "Help me persuade the authorities to turn the baby over to me. You know I'll take good care of her."

He rubbed his hands over his face, then gazed deeply into her eyes. "Do you understand that this is not my daughter?" His voice was compelling.

She knew the answer he wanted. He wanted her to say, "Yes, I believe you,' but she couldn't. She was still too unsure.

"I understand that is your statement" was the best she could do.

She saw the flash of disappointment that crossed his face before he erased it.

"Oh, hell," he muttered crossly and stood. "Do whatever you want to do, all of you. I'm going home."

The following morning Rick called Jodi with a terse message. "I've arranged for you to take temporary custody of the baby," he said impersonally. "I've also talked to Dr. Sam, and he's agreed to meet us at the hospital at eleven o'clock. Since you don't have a car seat for the little one I'll pick you up and then drive you and the baby home. Okay?"

Jodi's joy was dampened by Rick's aloofness, but she was determined not to let it bother her.

"That's wonderful!" she said enthusiastically, ignoring his coolness. "I'll be ready and waiting for you, and...thank you, Rick. I know you don't approve—"

"Are you absolutely sure this is what you want to do?" he interrupted brusquely.

"Oh, yes. I'm positive," she assured him.

"Then it's no longer any of my business," he told her and hung up.

Jodi was ready to go and watching out the window when Rick drove up to the house, but she didn't go outside to meet him. Instead, she waited for him to come in, hoping his mother could soften his disapproval, but it didn't happen. He greeted Dorothy, asked Jodi if she was ready to leave and escorted her out to the car, all very cold and formal.

Since he had made it plain he didn't want to talk, she had nothing but her own thoughts for company. Why did he disapprove so strongly of her caring for the baby? Was it because he didn't want her to extend her stay in Copper Canyon? But why would that matter to him one way or the other?

Or was he still sensitive to the possibility that people would believe the child was his because it was being cared for in his parents' home? If so, she could still rent an apartment and move, although Dorothy would be severely disappointed. She was so looking forward to having a baby in the house again.

A third possibility, and the most chilling, was that he disliked children so much that he didn't want to be confronted by one every time he visited his parents. Could the Richard McBride she knew and loved really be that self-centered and intolerant? If that was the case, then maybe he was the child's father after all, and didn't want the constant reminder!

She was shaken out of her unhappy thoughts when Rick

turned the car into the hospital parking lot and shut off the engine.

At the registration desk Rick inquired about Dr. Sam and was told he was in the building and had left instructions that he'd meet them in "Baby Doe's room."

"Baby Doe" indeed, Jodi thought indignantly. It was time that child had a proper name, and she guessed it was up to her to give it one.

They found her sound asleep. Unable to resist touching her, Jodi leaned over the crib and ran her palm gently over the down covered little head. "Oh, you sweet little thing," she murmured. "How could anybody not want you?"

She felt tears gathering in her eyes and rubbed at them with her fingers as she straightened up and almost bumped into Rick.

"Jodi, don't," he entreated. "Don't get so emotionally involved with this child. It could break your heart."

They were standing so close together that the back of her jacket touched the front of his. She had to force herself not to lean back against his strong hard chest. Would he put his arms around her if she did? The very thought sent a wave of heat through her. Or, more likely, would he just stand there and tolerate it?

The decision was taken away from her by Dr. Sam's voice in the doorway. "Sorry to keep you waiting, but I've got a patient in the last stage of labor."

He came into the room as Rick stepped away from Jodi and turned to him. "Sam, is there any chance this baby could be one you delivered?"

Sam shook his head. "No way! This infant was delivered without medical assistance. No physician would have tied the umbilical cord with a dirty string and then done such a botched-up job of cutting it. Also, neither my assistant nor I have delivered a child in almost a month. This one is nowhere near that old, and she's not premature enough to have been delivered by any of our other maternity patients.

Besides, all our mothers are looking forward to their babies."

"Would you mind checking the hospital in Grangeville, and any others you may know of around here, for me to see if a woman has come into emergency for postpartum care?"

This time he nodded. "Sure. No problem. I'll check Boise and Lewiston, too. The information will be on the computer. Now, let's get this little lady ready to go home."

He looked at Jodi. "I understand you're going to take care of her until she's placed in a permanent home?"

Jodi grinned broadly. "Yes, I am. I gather you put in a good word for me?" She knew the child welfare people would never have approved her if the doctor had objected.

He grinned, too. "Sure did. After all, you came highly recommended by my old pal, Rick, here."

That really startled her, and she glanced at Rick but he turned away, pretending he didn't see.

"Except for an infection of the umbilical cord area, which can be easily treated, she's perfectly healthy," the doctor told Jodi. "Her blood tests are clear, no drugs or signs of disease. You can take her home in the clothes she has on, and I've told the nurse to find a blanket you can wrap her up in. I left a folder at the nurses' station for you containing instructions for a formula, a booklet of advice on caring for newborns and medication for her navel. You can pick it up when you check her out. Any questions?"

Jodi smiled. "Not now, but as soon as I get her home I'm sure I'll have a million of them."

Sam laughed. "If you do, ask Dorothy. She knows just about everything there is to know concerning the care and feeding of babies, but should you have a question she can't answer don't hesitate to call my office. If I'm not there they can get ahold of me."

He looked at Rick. "I'll have my secretary get right on

that hospital search for new mothers who have delivered in the past forty-eight hours or so. Meanwhile, good luck.''

The next few days went by in a blur of excitement and exhaustion. Jodi had decided against giving the baby a permanent name since her future adoptive parents would want to do that, but instead called her Dolly because she was such a little doll.

Unfortunately, Jodi's sweet little Dolly had somehow gotten her days and nights mixed up. She slept during the day and loudly demanded attention all night, which left Jodi a little bleary-eyed and inclined to sleep when the baby did.

Dorothy and Shawn were delighted with Dolly, too, and they insisted on buying the furniture she needed, such as a crib and baby carrier. Jodi supplied the layette, blankets, bottles, etc., and reveled in selecting the tiny garments.

Dr. Sam had had no luck in tracking down the infant's mother through hospital records in the area, and there'd been no missing person reports that might fit.

However, there was one glitch in their paradise. Rick hadn't been over to visit his parents since he'd dropped Jodi and the baby off at the house on Tuesday. At first Jodi had been too busy shopping and adjusting to Dolly's routine to notice, but by Monday she was not only aware of his absence but alarmed by it.

She'd also had time to think about her attitude toward him, and decided that she'd been grossly unfair to just assume that the baby's mother was telling the truth. Jodi hadn't even considered that the woman was the one who was lying, not Rick.

This realization haunted her more and more each day until she finally accepted the fact that she owed him an apology. If he wasn't Dolly's father, he had every right to resent her lack of faith in him, and she knew she had to set things straight.

Not only because this misunderstanding between them

was also affecting his relationship with his parents, but because she loved him and wanted to resolve their estrangement. The picture in her mind of the pain in his expression when she'd accused him of lying tormented her day and night, and she couldn't bear it any longer. It was time she had a talk with him!

Before she could reconsider she picked up the phone, dialed the police station and asked for him. "Just a moment," the dispatcher said, and in a few seconds he came on the line.

"Rick, this is Jodi," she said in response to his terse hello.

There was a moment of silence on the other end, then, "Hello, Jodi. What can I do for you?"

You can love me, she thought, but quickly banished it.

"I need to talk to you," she said. "Would this evening be convenient?"

"Is something wrong?" This time he sounded alarmed.

"No," she hurried to assure him, then paused. "Well...yes, but it's not urgent. If you're busy—"

"Barring an emergency I'll be free by seven," he told her briskly. "Where do you want to meet?"

He sounded so stiff and businesslike. Maybe this wasn't a good idea, after all. Still, it was too late to back out now.

"I...I'd like to come to your house. That is, if that's all right with you," she stammered.

There was another slight pause, then, "Fine. Is seven okay?"

She nodded, then realized he couldn't see the gesture. "Yes, thank you. I...I won't bring the baby."

That last sentence was a mistake. "Dammit, Jodi, don't pussyfoot around. That's not my kid," he exploded. "I don't care one way or the other whether you bring her with you."

She drew a deep breath. "Rick, please, I didn't mean... Oh, never mind. I'll be there at seven." She hung up.

* * *

True to her word Jodi arrived at Rick's front porch exactly at seven o'clock that evening and rang the bell. There were lights on so he must be home. She'd explained her problem with Rick to his mother and asked her if she could watch Dolly for a short time while Jodi tried to placate him.

Dorothy was not only willing but eager to have the baby all to herself, and had encouraged Jodi to spend as much time with Rick as she needed to make things right between them.

She heard his heavy, booted footsteps before he opened the door. He didn't smile, but neither did he look as grim as she'd become accustomed to. He'd changed out of his uniform and was wearing brown slacks and a loose-fitting fawn print shirt. He looked so...so virile that it took her breath away, and she was glad he spoke first.

"Come in, Jodi." He stepped back to allow her to enter without either of them touching, then shut the door behind her. "Give me your coat and I'll hang it up."

She'd alerted friends and employers in Cincinnati that she would be staying in Copper Canyon indefinitely, and had asked her best friend to send her some more of her clothes. They'd arrived that morning, and she was glad to have her long heavy leaf green dress coat. It was warm and also very attractive.

He helped her shrug out of it, and underneath it she wore a short gray wool skirt and a soft pink cashmere sweater. She saw the admiration in Rick's expressive brown eyes before he blinked it away.

"We'll talk in the living room," he said and turned to lead the way. "It's nice and warm in there with the fire blazing."

He was right. It was toasty and snug with the crackle of the flames and the lights turned low. Inviting and seductive. Had he planned this to be romantic because she was coming, or was it always so? She'd never been in Rick's house at night before.

She hoped he'd set it up especially for her, but she doubted it. He didn't look in the mood for love.

He motioned for her to sit down, then walked over to the bar in one corner. "What will you have to drink?"

She really didn't want a drink; she needed to keep her wits about her. But on the other hand it might calm her frazzled nerves. "A screwdriver, please."

He nodded and reached for the vodka. "So how are you getting along with the baby?" he asked conversationally.

"Just great!" she said, trying to temper her enthusiasm while picking her words carefully so as not to antagonize him again. "We call her Dolly for want of a proper name, and she's a little love. Why don't you come over and see for yourself?"

He frowned. "Now look," he snapped. "If you're insinuating that I'm neglecting my own child, I—"

"That's not what I'm doing," she protested. "I was just issuing an invitation. I hoped you might be interested."

He flushed and looked down. "I've been busy."

Her heart sank, but she'd already put her foot in her mouth so she might as well go all the way. "So busy that you can't even find time to stop by and say hello to your dad and mom?"

"My relationship with my parents is just fine, thank you," he said curtly, "and how does it concern you, anyway?"

He stirred the vodka and orange juice, then poured whiskey over the ice cubes in a second glass.

"You know how it concerns me," she retorted. "If Dolly and I weren't living there you'd be in and out all the time. Are you trying to drive me away? Is that it?"

He put down the whiskey bottle, then picked up the two glasses and some napkins and headed across the room toward her.

"I don't know. Maybe I am," he admitted wearily as he handed her the screwdriver. "I'm as fallible as any man. Maybe I can only take so much before I start to run and hide."

He walked to the other end of the long sofa from her and sank down into the cushion.

His capitulation was unexpected. "Take so much of what?" she gasped.

"Look, Jodi, I don't need this," he said. "It's been a rough week and I'm not up to bantering insults with you. If all you came over here for was to tell me what a rotten person I am in general, and father and son in particular, then please, just go home and leave me alone. You've got the baby. That's what you wanted, isn't it, so don't ask anything else of me."

She could only stare at him, speechless. Did he really believe she thought so badly of him?

Yes, of course he did, and it was her own fault. All she'd done since she found the baby on his doorstep was to criticize him and make it plain she didn't believe anything he said.

That hadn't been her intention, but obviously that was the way it had come across to him, and she was heartily ashamed of herself. Who was she to judge him? He'd never been anything but kind and considerate to her until she started needling him all the time.

She took a long drink of her screwdriver, then leaned foreword and set the glass on the coffee table. Her hands were shaking, and she spilled a little of it. With the cocktail napkin he'd brought her she wiped up the liquid, then stood, walked to the other end of the sofa and sat down beside him, so close that their thighs touched.

He glared at her, startled, and she was tempted to move away. She wasn't used to taking the lead with a man, but she was determined to get this misunderstanding cleared up.

"Rick," she said softly, "I don't want to fight with you. I came over to apologize for ever doubting you. I know you're an honorable man."

She felt his thigh muscles twitch against her leg, but he didn't give an inch. He took a long swallow of his whiskey, then set his glass down, too. "You could have fooled me," he muttered.

"I was wrong," she admitted. "But even though the baby was left on your doorstep it never occurred to me that you might be her father until I found the note."

She reached for his hand and clasped it between both of hers. "When that happened I went off the deep end. I realize that now and I'm truly sorry, but I just couldn't conceive of a woman abandoning her newborn child on any man's doorstep and leaving a note naming him as the father if he wasn't."

Moving the hand she was holding to his chest she felt his rapid heartbeat. She leaned closer and murmured against his ear. "Does your heart always beat so fast?"

With a quick flip of the wrist he clasped one of her hands and pressed it against his chest directly over the pounding organ. "Are you deliberately tormenting me, Jodi?" His tone was anguished.

"*Am* I tormenting you?" Her own voice shook.

"You know damn well you are." It was more of a purr than a complaint.

She rubbed her cheek against his. "Do you want me to stop?"

He groaned and put his arms around her. "Oh, God no," he murmured and buried his face in the side of her neck. "Don't ever stop. I don't think I could stand it if you did."

That made her own heart leap with joy. She put her arms around him and stroked the back of his head. "You look so tired," she said softly.

"I am." His lips and his warm breath against her neck made her shiver. "I haven't been sleeping much."

"Because of me?" she asked when he didn't elaborate.

"Mostly."

She was sorry he'd lost sleep over her, but she was glad, too, and encouraged. God knows, he'd haunted her dreams often enough.

"Why didn't you tell me?" she asked as her stroking hands moved down to his shoulders.

His arms tightened around her and now she could feel his heart pounding against hers. "Because men are supposed to be strong and suffer in silence," he muttered.

"Isn't that sort of stupid?" she chided.

She felt his tight muscles start to relax as her fingers gently massaged them.

"Apparently so," he agreed on a sigh. "If I had come to you would you have helped me to sleep?"

A teasing grin hovered on her lips. "Eventually," she whispered seductively.

Chapter Eleven

Rick was almost overwhelmed with conflicting emotions. Love and anxiety, desire and caution, gratitude and distrust, joy and depression. This tantalizing woman in his arms who was playing him like a harp had turned his world upside down in the month she'd been in Copper Canyon.

He'd known from the first minute he saw her she was going to be trouble because of the strong surge of feeling she'd aroused in him just by walking through the door of the police station. He'd never had that much of a reaction to a woman on first sight before.

Jodi had put him through purgatory, not only this past week but ever since that first night she got here when he said goodbye to her in his parents' entry hall. He'd had an almost irresistible urge to take her in his arms and kiss her. It had cost him dearly to resist and had set off short bursts of fire in his blood that started a blaze he'd never been able to put out.

Now she was stoking the flames, and he was powerless to stop her. On the contrary, he doubted if he'd ever be able to let her go. He needed her in his arms, in his bed, in his life, and for now he wasn't going to think about why he couldn't have her.

She stirred in his embrace, and instinctively he crushed her closer, afraid she'd pull away from him. Instead, she reached under his loose shirt and rubbed her soft little hands over his bare back, eliciting a moan of exquisite agony from deep in his throat.

Did she know what she was doing to him? Of course she did. She was a grown woman, not an adolescent.

Unable to resist any longer he put his hand on her breast. The soft fiber of the cashmere sweater was almost as enticing as the full rise of flesh beneath it, and he discovered that she wasn't wearing a bra.

She fit into his palm as if she'd been made to its measurements, and she caught her breath as her fingers dug into his overheated skin.

His thumbs were big and strong, and he had to remind himself to be careful not to hurt her as he rolled her nipple with one and felt it harden.

She was almost as turned on as he. How he wanted her!

Slowly he let his hand roam over her rib cage to her waist, then steal under her sweater where it made contact with her warm, soft, bare flesh. Much to his consternation her muscles contracted and he ceased all movement.

"I'm sorry, love," he said anxiously. "Do you want me to stop?"

Her fingers were doing magical things to his back, and her voice quivered when she answered. "Oh, no, please don't. That was a twinge of pleasure, not pain."

He breathed a sigh of relief and resumed his explorations. When he reached her bare breast he again cupped it, but this time without the intrusion of the sweater. It was high, and full, and her nipple was still hard and peaked. Her heart was pounding in time with his own, and he felt as if he were going to explode.

If he didn't break this off soon there'd be no turning back!

He raised his head to tell her so, but then found his face only inches from hers. Her wide blue eyes were dark and misty with need, and her full lips trembled. Without his willing it his mouth opened to cover hers and he was lost.

She tasted of orange juice and woman, and her talented tongue danced and played with his in a crescendo of sensations. The hand that wasn't caressing her breast skimmed down her skirt to her nylon-covered thigh. It felt firm and round and rocked when he gently kneaded it.

He was so aroused that it was actually painful. The bottom of her skirt only barely covered her hips when she was sitting, and she offered no objection when he inched his hand slowly underneath it and found her panty-hose-covered derriere.

It, too, was firm but giving, and he silently cursed the makers of the confining garment. He could strip it off her easily enough, and was sorely tempted to do so, but the nearly mute voice of his ignored conscience warned him not to. Flimsy though it was, it acted as a barrier to his nearly uncontrollable desire. A barrier he desperately needed unless he was prepared to accept the consequences of seducing her when he knew he could never marry her.

It took all the willpower he could muster to draw his hand out from beneath her skirt and break off the kiss. "Jodi, this has got to stop," he said in a tone that was more like a plea than a command.

She blinked, and he noticed that her lips were swollen from his kisses. "You don't like it?" She looked as if he'd slapped her.

How could she possibly think that? He gathered her close again. "Of course I like it, sweetheart! That's the problem, I like it too much. I'm only human, after all. Another two seconds and I'd have torn your clothes off and made love to you right here on the sofa!"

She still looked disbelieving. "Would that have been so bad?"

He sighed with regret. "It would have been wonderful," he murmured softly, "but it would also be disastrous. I won't change my mind about giving you children, and you know you could never be happy in a relationship that didn't include them."

He kissed the tip of her patrician nose and the cleft of her chin, but astutely avoided her pouting lips. If he even grazed them, he'd be lost. "I'm sorry. I wish I felt different but I don't, and I never will. It's too big a problem to ignore, and it can never be resolved."

Jodi's disappointment turned to annoyance. What did he have against children? And how could he be so sure that he'd never change his mind? He had all the attributes of a good father, but he wouldn't give himself a chance to explore them. He shied away from children. Wouldn't even visit the baby that had been left on his doorstep. Obviously Dolly's mother thought he was daddy material. She'd left her child with him!

She straightened up and pulled away from him. "It's getting late," she said inanely and stood. "I didn't intend to stay so long. I don't want to impose further on your mom to take care of the baby."

She started to walk toward the door, but Rick caught up with her and put his arms around her waist from behind. "Jodi." His voice was strained and filled with regret. "Please don't be mad at me. Can we at least be friends?"

She melted like butter held over a flame and leaned back against him. What he asked didn't seem likely. With the magnetism that radiated between them they could be lovers or they could be antagonists, but she wouldn't bet on their chances of being just friends.

However, she was willing to try. It was better than nothing.

"I don't know, Rick," she said mournfully. "How's your self-control?"

He rubbed his cheek in her hair. "Practically nonexistent."

"So is mine, but I'm willing to try if you are. That is, for the sake of your relationship with your parents," she amended to salvage a remnant of her shattered pride.

Things between them were different for the next couple of days. Rick came to his parents' house for lunch the following noon. Little Dolly slept, and Jodi didn't suggest that he go upstairs and look at her. He was friendly and impersonal with Jodi, but the sexual tension between them was uncomfortable.

On the second day he didn't come over but called and chatted with her on the phone for a few minutes. He even asked about the baby and how she was getting along.

On the third day, Friday, Jodi had a phone call from a man who introduced himself as Bob Kelly. "I'm chief of the volunteer fire department here in Copper Canyon," he told her. "I understand you owned the Coldwell house that burned down the other night?"

Jodi frowned and wondered what could have gone wrong now. "Yes, I did. However, it was up for sale, and I've since sold the property."

There was a pause. "I see, but it was still in your name at the time of the fire, wasn't it?"

"Yes. Is something the matter?"

"I'm afraid so," Chief Kelly said. "I've been getting complaints about the unsightly rubble out there. Are you planning to have it torn down and hauled away soon?"

Jodi was becoming more perplexed by the minute. "You mean it hasn't been cleaned up yet?"

"No, ma'am, it hasn't," he said forcefully, "and the neighbors are getting pretty hot about it. They claim it's an attractive nuisance for their children, and they're right. I've just been out to inspect it, and it's not only an eyesore but a dangerous one. Someone could get hurt."

"But I don't understand," Jodi said. "I sold it to Finch Realty a few days after the fire with the provision that they have it cleaned off. I haven't seen or heard from Mr. Finch since."

"Mmm," the chief murmured. "Apparently neither has anyone else. I saw the For Sale sign on the property before the fire, so yesterday I called Farley to find out who owns it. His secretary told me he's been out of town on a family matter, and she doesn't know when he'll be back. She gave me your name as the owner."

Jodi was thoroughly confused. "I don't know why she wouldn't know that I sold it. I signed the contract right there in Mr. Finch's office."

"That's mighty odd," Chief Kelly exclaimed. "If I were you, I'd look into it, Ms. Hopkins. I'm not a lawyer, but I suspect that until the transaction is completed you can be held responsible if anyone is hurt on the property."

"I'll check it out immediately," she assured him, "and thanks for bringing it to my attention. I'll let you know what I find out."

"Thank you, ma'am. I'd appreciate it."

As soon as the connection was broken Jodi called Rick and repeated the conversation to him. "I just don't understand," she concluded. "Farley was in such a hurry to get the property on the market again that he even bought it from me himself for resale even though he knew it would probably cost more to clear off than he could make on it. Now I find out he hasn't cleaned it up or told his staff that the realty owns it."

"His so-called staff consists of just his secretary, but it is strange," Rick agreed. "Let me check around and see what I can discover. I'll call Victor and find out just what your legal status is in regard to the property, then take it from there."

She lowered her voice to a husky drawl. "Thank you, Rick, I knew I could count on you."

"Always, sweetheart," he said huskily. "You just take care of the baby and let me worry about straightening this thing out."

A warm feeling stole over her. He talked as if they were a family, all three of them.

Or was she just fantasizing again?

The following morning Rick woke with an agenda already fixed in his mind. Although it was Saturday and technically his day off he was going to start tracking down Farley Finch and find out just what in hell was going on.

A glance out the window told him that the first snow of the season had arrived in all its cold winter majesty. The ground was white and the silent flakes were falling fast. He shivered and turned up the heat on the thermostat.

After a shower and a hasty breakfast he was just leaving the house when the phone rang. With a sigh he shut the door and went to answer it, hoping it wasn't someone reporting an accident on the icy roads.

It wasn't. It was the hospital in Grangeville. "We have a patient here who was admitted last night," he was told. "She says her name is Blossom and she's demanding to see you."

"Me?" Rick asked, surprised. "I don't know anyone named Blossom. What's her last name?"

"She won't say," the spokeswoman replied. "Blossom is apparently her street name. She appears to be homeless. Her condition is critical, and I'd advise you to come as soon as possible if you want to talk to her. The prognosis is poor."

He scowled. A glimmer of light was beginning to dawn. "How old is she and what's wrong with her?"

"She says she's eighteen, but she looks younger. There are numerous things wrong with her including malnutrition and bronchitis, but the most serious is an infection caused from giving birth unattended and with no follow-up post-partum care."

Sweet Lord, she must be baby Dolly's mother!

"I'll be there in half an hour or less," he said brusquely and broke the connection, then dialed his parents' number.

Rick's car roared into the Grangeville hospital parking lot twenty-five minutes later, but he wasn't alone. He had Jodi with him. He'd called and invited her to come, and she'd been waiting on the sidewalk when he got to the house, as eager as he to hear what the young woman had to say.

At the registration desk they were directed to the intensive care unit on the second floor, and Rick asked that a stenographer be sent up to take notes. Dr. Paul Nolan, whom Rick knew well, was waiting for him on the second floor, and Rick introduced him to Jodi. "Is it okay if she comes in the room with me? She's taking care of the baby whom I suspect belongs to this woman."

The doctor nodded and looked at Jodi. "That's all right, but stay back and let Rick do the talking. She's very weak."

They were outfitted with white gowns and masks before all three entered the room that had two beds but only one patient, a girl who surely wasn't more than sixteen. Her mousy brown hair was stringy and her complexion had a pasty gray cast. Her eyes were closed and her breathing, even with the oxygen, was shallow and raspy.

Rick could see that the doctor was right. Her chances for survival looked mighty slim.

The poor kid, he thought. No wonder she left her baby on his porch for him to find. She was in no shape to take care of anyone, not even herself, but why had she named him as the father? And why wasn't she in school instead of wandering around the country homeless and abused?

He heard Jodi's quick intake of breath and wished he hadn't subjected her to this. She was so tenderhearted. This was going to be torture for her, but he knew she wouldn't leave.

One thing he was positive of. None of Jodi's children would ever end up in this condition! She'd give them all the tender loving care any child would need.

A wave of bitter regret swept over him. Dear God, if only...if only...

He was startled out of his reverie by the sound of someone entering the room, and he turned to see a middle-aged woman also outfitted in a white gown and mask carrying a notebook and pen. The stenographer. Now they could begin.

He motioned her to pull up a chair and sit down near the top of the other side of the bed. Paul and Jodi stood at the bottom.

Rick leaned over and touched the girl's pitifully bony shoulder. "Blossom," he called softly. He wasn't sure if she was asleep or unconscious.

When she didn't respond he called her name again and shook her shoulder very gently.

Slowly her eyelids fluttered, then opened to reveal dull blue eyes with no luster. The eyes of a tormented soul in pain.

"Blossom," he said carefully. "I'm Rick McBride. Police Chief McBride from Copper Canyon. You asked to speak to me?"

She closed her eyes again, as if the burden of keeping them open was too great. "Yes," she said, barely above a whisper. "I left my baby with you."

That came as no surprise at all to Rick. "Yes, you did. Can you tell me about the baby? Was it a boy or a girl?"

This time her eyes opened wide with alarm. "Didn't you find her?" Her voice was filled with panic.

He patted her shoulder reassuringly. "I found the baby

and it's fine, but I need to be sure we're both talking about the same child."

She looked perplexed. "Do...do women leave their babies on your porch often?" she asked in all seriousness.

He glanced at Paul and saw the big lug's eyes twinkle with amusement. Rick would have words with the jolly doctor later.

"No, it's never happened before," he assured her, "but these questions are necessary so we can give your baby the best possible care. Now, was it a boy or a girl?"

She seemed satisfied, and once more closed her eyes. "A girl," she murmured wearily.

"When was she born?"

It was several seconds before she answered. "Don't know date—same day I left her on your porch."

Rick glanced over at the steno to make sure she was getting this all down. She was.

"Fine," he said. "Can you tell me where she was born?"

"In a motel room. I...I cleaned it up good afterward," she hastened to assure them.

Rick's heart nearly broke, and he heard Jodi sob. Damn it to hell! Where were the people who were supposed to be taking care of this girl who was little more than a child herself?

He cleared his throat to make sure his voice was under control. "I'm sure you did," he said and took her hand, the one that wasn't strapped to an IV tube. "What was the name of the motel?"

Again it was a while before she answered. "Don't remember. I'd been working there as a cleaning lady. Didn't pay much, but they...they let me stay in one of the rooms."

Again Jodi sobbed. Rick looked at her and saw tears streaming down her stricken face. He made a mental note to find the bastards who would take advantage of a sick and pregnant teenager and deal with them personally.

"Blossom, where do your parents live? Where is your home? What's your real name?"

A tear rolled from behind her closed eyelids, and she clamped her lips together and shook her head. Her message was clear. She wasn't going to talk about her past life.

The doctor glanced at the monitor above the bed. "That's enough for now," he said firmly. "Her strength is severely limited."

"Can I ask just one more question, Paul?" Rick said anxiously. "I promise not to push if she's not up to answering."

Paul thought for a moment, then nodded. "Okay, but make it short."

Rick leaned over the bed and spoke softly. "Blossom, why did you leave the baby at my house and indicate in the note that I am her father?"

She opened her eyes again and looked at him. "S-sorry." Her voice was very weak. "Had to leave her with someone who'd take care of her. You...you're well-known in town... Heard everyone talk about how nice you are... I checked you out."

She closed her eyes again. "You were single," she continued after a moment, "came from a close-knit family...had a good job."

Her breathing was becoming more labored, and again she paused briefly. "I—I hoped...if you thought you were the baby's father you'd keep her and raise her...at least see that she was placed in a home with people who would love her..."

She was interrupted by a fit of coughing, and the doctor stepped in. "That's it, Rick," he said in a tone that was meant to be obeyed. "No more. I want all of you to clear out of here now. My patient needs rest."

The stenographer stood and joined Jodi as they both left the room, but Rick hung back. The cough had stopped and Blossom was again lying quietly.

He stroked a lock of damp hair off her forehead and leaned down closer to murmur in her ear. "I promise you, Blossom, I'll take care of *our* little girl and see that she's adopted into a nice home with loving parents."

He emphasized the "our," hoping she'd understand that he was taking on the role of father in finding her daughter a good home.

For the first time a tiny smile lifted the corners of her mouth. "I knew you would," she told him, just before her eyes closed again in sleep.

Chapter Twelve

In the hall outside the intensive care room Jodi fought to control her sobs and swiped at her wet cheeks with the back of her hand. One of the nurses handed her a box of tissues and she took one and blew her nose.

She'd barely managed to stop the tears when Rick came out of the room, glanced at her, then took her in his arms, and the tears started flowing all over again.

"I'm sorry, Jodi," he said as he held her close. "I never should have brought you with me. I had no idea...or rather I just didn't think..."

She lifted her head from his shoulder. "I'm glad you brought me," she assured him. "I'm just sorry I'm such a crybaby—"

"You're a sweet and loving woman, that's what you are," he corrected. "That poor girl—" His voice broke, and Jodi knew he was fighting his own heartache.

"Come on, let's get out of here," he said gruffly. "We can do more for her by seeing that her daughter is taken care of than we can just sitting around here getting in the way."

They didn't talk again until they were in the car and on their way back to Copper Canyon. By that time Jodi had managed to pull herself together and think straight.

"Do you believe there's any chance of finding Blossom's parents?" she asked Rick.

"Not much," he said, "but even if we could I'm not sure we should."

Jodi was shocked. "But why? They must be worried sick about her. Don't you think they have a right to know they have a baby granddaughter?"

Rick glanced at her. "That depends on why she apparently ran away." His voice was grim. "Children seldom run away from understanding and loving parents. Blossom obviously doesn't want to be found. She refused to tell me anything about her past, even now that she has a newborn baby and is so sick. I'll run her fingerprints and see what I can come up with, but even if I find out who her parents are, I'm not going to contact them unless she gives her permission."

Jodi was shocked. "But don't they have the right to know?"

"Not if Blossom's of legal age, and doesn't want them to," he told her. "There's no law that says adults can't disappear if they want to. She gave her age as eighteen and I'm going to take her word for it unless I find out otherwise."

The following day the dilemma was resolved. Dr. Nolan called Rick to tell him Blossom had died peacefully during the night.

With the mystery of Dolly's origins cleared up, the infant was now eligible for adoption, and Jodi began girding herself to give up the child. There were a number of couples waiting to adopt, so there would be no problem placing her in a good home.

The thought of giving Dolly up was almost too painful

to bear, but Jodi had always known that was inevitable and she vowed to enjoy every minute of the time she had left with the baby. She also knew that her stay in Copper Canyon was rapidly approaching the end. There was no longer any excuse for it. Rick popped in often to visit with her and his parents, but the two of them were never alone together.

She was dreaming an impossible dream, and the sooner she got back to the reality of Cincinnati, the better.

Then Rick found Farley Finch!

The real estate agent hadn't been seen since the Monday after the fire when he'd agreed to buy Jodi's property and then disappeared without completing the transaction. Even his secretary hadn't heard from him, and he had no wife or family.

A little detective work on Rick's part turned him up in Boise, where he was staying in a cheap motel and getting treatment for severe burns on the upper part of his body. He readily admitted setting the fire, and a great deal more. With the help of the Boise police Rick arrested him and brought him back to Copper Canyon to stand trial on charges of arson and fraud as well as several more minor ones.

"It was the damnedest thing," Rick told Dorothy, Shawn and Jodi that night in his parents' living room. "Everyone in town knows that Farley has always operated on the ragged edge of the law, but he was never caught doing anything actually illegal until now. It seems that he learned through his statewide real estate contacts that a big development corporation plans to build a shopping mall in that area where your property is, Jodi."

"Really?" they all three chorused.

"That's something we badly need," Dorothy said enthusiastically. "There's no decent place to shop this side of Boise or Lewiston."

"Right," Rick said. "It will attract shoppers from all over and make the corporation a ton of money. They'll also pay whatever price they have to for that land. That's why their plans have been kept under wraps until they are ready to start acquiring it. They naturally wanted to get it as cheap as they could, but when Farley found out about it he passed the word on to Harlan Lowery at the bank and several other 'financial speculators' of the town.

"They formed a silent partnership and have been buying up the run-down property at rock-bottom prices so they can sell it to the developers at inflated prices when they start negotiating for the land."

"But Lowery and the bank are the executors of my aunt's estate!" Jodi protested. "Isn't that illegal?"

Rick grinned. "Yes, darlin', it certainly is. Lowery's in double trouble for defrauding an estate he was managing as well as defrauding the other homeowners."

Jodi blinked. "Then I was right. My property is worth more than what Farley offered to pay for it?"

Rick nodded. "Much more. Especially so if he had managed to pull off his grand scheme. The owners' corporation could have made the developers pay dearly for that land after they picked it up for practically nothing."

Jodi still didn't understand. "But why did Farley burn the house down?"

Rick chuckled. "It seems that you were the only owner who refused to sell to them, and they couldn't offer you more money for fear the other owners who had sold cheap would hear about it and become suspicious."

His smile disappeared and he was all seriousness. "The wanna-be buyers were the ones responsible for breaking in and trashing your house, as well as spreading the rumors that it was haunted. They figured that would scare you off, and you'd sell at their price just to get rid of it. Oh, they're also being charged with conspiracy."

"But the fire—" Jodi prodded.

"I'm coming to that," Rick interrupted. "The fire was a last-ditch effort to scare you away. One of the other investors had agreed to set it, but he backed out at the last moment, so Farley did it himself. The problem was that he didn't know anything about setting fires, and he used too much flammable liquid, then lit it with a cigarette lighter. The fire flared up and out of control before he could get out, and he was burned."

"How awful!" Dorothy murmured.

"Served the bastard right," Rick muttered unsympathetically. "Anyway, he went to Lowery, who gave him first aid and drove him to a hospital in Boise."

"But he was here that Monday..." Jodi faltered. "That must be why he seemed so uncomfortable. He was wearing loose-fitting clothes, too, and I remember wondering about it."

"I'm sure he was uncomfortable," Rick said. "He was probably in agony, but he couldn't go to a doctor here in town. Everyone would know burns of that magnitude had to have been tied to the fire. He must have come back here for his appointment with you, then driven right back to Boise after you left him and has been there ever since. He wouldn't dare come home until the burns were pretty well healed."

Jodi breathed a sigh of relief. At last that nasty business was cleared up. "Will Farley and Harlan and their co-conspirators be punished?"

"Oh, yes," Rick assured her. "I expect they'll spend several years in prison, and for the rest of their lives they'll have a felony conviction hanging over their heads. I'd say they have a pretty bleak future to look forward to."

A short while later Rick stood and announced that it was time for him to leave. Jodi put on her coat and walked with him to his car. It was a beautiful night, cold but bright with the moonbeams bouncing off the snow.

They stopped on the curb, and Rick reached out and put

his arms around her. "You know I can't resist you," he murmured and cuddled her close.

"I'd say you do a masterful job of resisting me," she replied, and buried her cold face against his sheepskin jacket.

"Then you'd be wrong." His breath was warm against her ear. "If I did what I ache to do I'd take you home with me and we'd spend the night making love."

He talked a real good game. If only he'd play it, too.

"But you're not going to do that, are you." She didn't bother to make a question of it.

"No, I'm not," he said raggedly, "and once you get back to Ohio you'll thank me for it."

It was no use. He might want her, even need her, but he didn't love her. If he did he'd stop using his aversion to children as an excuse to send her away and start working on a way to overcome it. A lot of men who thought they never wanted children were the proudest fathers of all once they had one of their own.

She raised her head just as he lowered his, and their lips met and clung. His arms tightened and she put hers around his neck and opened to his invading tongue. She forgot the icy breeze. Her blood was warm enough to melt her protesting pride, and even through the heavy coats between them she could feel his hard and demanding passion.

Oh, Rick, why are you so damn stubborn? Why won't you give in and let us have just one night together before you send me away?

As if she'd spoken aloud he braced himself and set her apart from him, then walked around the car, got in and drove away.

The following day Jodi received an official notice from child welfare advising her that an adoptive family had been selected for Dolly, and she was being placed with them on Monday of the following week for a trial period. Jodi was instructed to bring the child to the Child Protection Agency at ten o'clock that morning, at which time her, Jodi's, services would be terminated.

She was alone in the house when the mail arrived, and she felt free to break down and cry as the searing pain of loss surged through her, but when the storm was over, she decided that was her last indulgence. She'd known her time with the baby would be short, and she wasn't going to make everyone around her miserable by brooding and feeling sorry for herself.

It was time to start planning her future. One that didn't include Rick and Dolly!

She didn't tell Rick's parents about the letter, but asked Dorothy if she could cook supper that night and invite Rick. Dorothy looked puzzled but readily agreed. So did he when she called and issued the invitation.

That evening she fixed the family's favorite chicken-and-broccoli casserole and served it with a garden salad, warm French bread with garlic butter and, for dessert, a chocolate cream pie that she picked up at the local bakery where everything tasted homemade.

Shortly before Rick arrived she changed into her plum-colored silk slacks suit, which should have clashed with her auburn hair but didn't. Instead, it accentuated the blue of her eyes and the creaminess of her complexion.

When Rick arrived, he put his hands at her waist and held her away from him, making no effort to hide his approval. "You're in the wrong business, love," he said huskily. "You could compete with any of those supermodels that appear in the fashion magazines."

Her heart melted and so did the rest of her as he gathered her in his arms and held her close while his parents watched.

"I'm glad you approve," she murmured shakily, then hugged him and stepped out of his embrace. She couldn't stand much of that without breaking down again.

Instead, she managed a happy smile. "Dinner will be ready in a few minutes, but meanwhile Shawn has agreed to act as bartender so just step up to the bar—" she added with a sweep of her hand as she indicated the kitchen counter, "and name your poison."

The meal was a happy one. Jodi forced herself to shove the announcement she would have to make later into the back of her mind and enjoy the food and the company.

Later, when their pie had been eaten and the table cleared they all settled down in the living room with after-dinner crème de menthe. Jodi and Rick sat together on the couch. Jodi's stomach muscles had begun to tighten with apprehension when she served the pie and now they were clenched into knots, but she couldn't put off what she had to do any longer.

After taking a swallow of her drink, she set it on the coffee table and cleared her throat. "Listen up, everybody," she said, trying for lightness. "I have something to share with you."

Rick and his dad stopped talking, and Dorothy glanced at her expectantly.

"This morning I received this in the mail." She held up the letter from Child Protection that she'd placed on the coffee table earlier. "I'd like to read it to you."

Everyone looked bewildered but no one spoke as she unfolded the notice, took a deep breath and read it out loud, being careful not to let her voice tremble.

For a moment after she finished, there was stunned silence, then Rick spoke. "Well, I...I guess we knew this would happen sooner or later." He watched Jodi carefully, and she knew he was waiting for her to cry. It was difficult to maintain her composure.

"But not so soon," Dorothy wailed. "Why, they've hardly had time to interview prospective adoptive parents, let alone do background checks and all."

"That would already have been done, honey," Shawn

told his wife. "They do that when a couple apply for a child to adopt, then the couple is put on a waiting list until one is available."

Rick nodded his agreement. "That's right, Mom. The couples are already cleared—it's just a matter of matching them up with a baby."

Again he looked at Jodi. "Are you all right, sweetheart?" He sounded worried.

"No, not really," she admitted. "I love that little girl, but she needs a permanent home with both a father and a mother, so I'm resigned to giving her up."

She fought to swallow a sob and only partially succeeded, but continued on, anyway. "It's also time I got on with my life, too, so I'm going to leave for Cincinnati as soon as I turn Dolly over to the Child Protection people."

The McBride family gaped at her, but none of them seemed able or willing to speak.

Jodi felt her lips tremble and clenched her fists in an effort to keep her voice steady. "I'll miss all of you. You've been like family to me, and I can never thank you enough for taking me in and making my stay here so...so enjoyable."

Her voice broke, and she cleared her throat. "I...I hope you'll come to Cincinnati sometime soon and see me. I'd love to show you around and introduce you to my friends—"

She realized she was rambling even before Dorothy cut her off. "Having you with us has been a pleasure, and we'll miss you terribly," she assured Jodi as she wiped her dewy eyes. "You're welcome here anytime."

The talk went on like that for the next several minutes, but Jodi was acutely aware that Rick had said nothing after she said she was leaving. He just sat with his glass in his hand and stared off into space. He didn't seem to be reacting to her announcement at all! Was he glad to be rid of both Dolly and her? She'd hoped he'd at least pretend he was sorry she was going away forever.

Chapter Thirteen

Rick felt as if he'd been kicked in the stomach. The pain hit him in waves, and he had to struggle just to breathe.

Jodi was leaving. Not some time in the distant future but now. In four more days she'd be gone.

He heard the regrets being voiced around him, but he couldn't even think, let alone speak. He'd known this was coming. There'd never been any doubt about it, but it was always nebulous. Sometime far off after he'd managed to convince himself that what he felt for her was just a passing attraction. It had been a long time since he'd had a woman. Given a little more time he'd really believe that this mixture of joy, sorrow, admiration and physical need that tormented him was just sexual hunger and would go away.

But time had just run out and the torment hadn't ceased. In fact, it was stronger than ever. He thought of her all day, dreamed of her at night and wanted her so bad it was like a burning thirst that couldn't be quenched.

What made it even more difficult was the fact that she had strong feelings for him, too. She'd let him know in such sweet ways that she wanted him, and the insistent need to turn her away was destroying him. She seemed to think that his refusal to father children was something he could control if he just tried hard enough. That was understandable, and it was his own fault. He'd led her to believe that, although it hadn't been his intention. He'd underestimated her keen intelligence and her persistence in going after what she wanted.

Maybe he should tell her the truth. That would wipe out any hopes she might have of changing his mind. He should have done that in the first place instead of pussyfooting around, but he'd also underestimated the depth of his feelings for her. He'd lived with his secret for thirteen years, and during all that time he'd seen no reason to reveal it to anyone. Certainly not a sexy young woman he had the hots for but who was only a passing fancy in his life.

Or so he'd mistakenly thought!

Gradually the veil of shock and misery that clouded his mind began to lift, and he became aware of the chatter of voices going on around him. Jodi was going back to Cincinnati. That was a given, but was he being unfair to her to let her go without knowing the real reason why he wouldn't marry her and give her children?

She'd honored him by letting him know she cared for him. Would he be dishonoring those tender sentiments by letting her leave thinking his feelings for her were so shallow that he'd give her up just because he didn't much care for children?

He wasn't sure, but he was going to find out!

Jodi was making polite conversation with Rick's parents, but she was acutely aware of his silent presence beside her on the couch. Why didn't he say something? Anything?

Almost as if she'd spoken aloud, he stood and turned to look down at her as he broke into the discussion. "Jodi, I need to talk to you." His tone was insistent. "Will you please come home with me now? We can bring the baby, too."

Jodi gasped. She'd been wishing he'd speak, but that was the last thing she'd expected him to say.

"I...that is, yes, I'll come with you," she managed to get out. "But Dolly's asleep and it's awfully cold to take her out so late."

He'd never before shown much interest in the child, so why was he now asking her and Dolly to go home with him?

Dorothy spoke up. "There's no need to disturb her. Your dad and I will be happy to baby-sit.

His attention was still concentrated on Jodi. "It's up to you, of course, but we can cover her with a heavy blanket. I'll warm up the car before we take her out, and she won't be exposed to the night air for more than a few seconds."

He sounded as if he really wanted her to bring the baby, and Jodi needed to know what had changed his mind about Dolly so suddenly.

"Thanks for your offer," she said to Dorothy, "but I think we can move her into the car bed without even disturbing her."

The car seat unfolded into an infant-sized bed, and they transferred her into it with hardly a ripple. Half an hour later they were in Rick's living room with a fire going in the fireplace and Dolly sound asleep, snuggled in her car bed on the floor beside the fire, close enough for warmth but far enough away for safety.

The only illumination in the room came from the seductive blaze, and Jodi wondered why Rick had brought her here where they were alone in such a romantic setting when he'd made it clear that he wasn't going to make love with her.

"Are you warm enough?" he asked as they sat down

together on the sofa, close but not touching. "I can turn the thermostat up."

She had a feeling she wasn't going to be just warm but steamy before this evening was over. "No, I'm fine, thanks."

After an awkward silence Rick spoke again. "You gave me quite a jolt tonight when you said you were going back to Cincinnati so soon."

Well, at least he'd been paying attention. "It's not sudden, Rick. I've been here much longer than I'd originally planned."

"I know, but the longer you stayed, the deeper I crawled into my fantasy that you'd never leave and you and I could be friends without being lovers."

She shook her head sadly. "I'm afraid that was pretty unrealistic."

"It was impossible," he retorted, "but I was too much in love with you to admit it. I kept telling myself—"

"In love?" Jodi couldn't believe what she was hearing. "Aren't you confusing love with lust?"

"Not for a minute," he insisted. "That's what's had me so spooked. I can handle lust, but I've never been in love before and it's turned my whole life upside down."

Jodi was totally unprepared for his admission, and it set off conflicting emotions in her that collided somewhere between her mind and her heart, leaving her shocked and speechless.

Her confusion must have been evident because he put his arms around her and drew her close. "I've been less than honest with you, sweetheart," he murmured into her hair. "I haven't told you the whole truth about why we can never have children."

Jodi cuddled against him and gave up trying to understand. He loved her and that was all that mattered. Surely if they loved each other any other problems could be worked out.

"Thirteen years ago when I was in college I got the mumps," he told her. "I was really sick and had to spend a few days in the hospital. Even when I got out I was still laid up for a while, but I gradually got my strength back and was able to resume my classes."

He paused as though reluctant to go on, and she raised her head to look at him. The look in his eyes was bleak and his face was twisted with pain.

Dear Lord, what had happened at that time to cause that much anguish so many years later?

"Rick, what happened!" It was a cry of fear, and she pulled away from him to straighten up. "What are you trying to tell me?"

He straightened, too, then got to his feet and walked over to hunker down beside Dolly in her portable car seat with his back to Jodi. "A few months later, at the doctor's suggestion, I had some tests done," he muttered.

Again he hesitated, and her fear and frustration mounted. Was there something gravely wrong with his health?

She jumped to her feet and went over to kneel on the floor beside them. "Rick, please, what kind of tests? What's wrong with you?"

He caressed the baby's face tenderly with his big hand, then turned his head and looked straight at Jodi. "That bout with the mumps left me sterile." His tone was as bleak as his eyes. "There's nothing wrong with my desire and ability to make love, but I can never be a father. It's not that I don't want to give you children, Jodi. I can't."

Jodi's sense of relief was so enormous that she scarcely felt the twinge of regret she shrugged off as she let out the breath she didn't know she'd been holding.

"Oh, is that all," she said gratefully.

Rick's eyes widened. "All! Don't you understand what

m saying? *I can't give you children!* It's not something ıat can be corrected or will go away in time. It's perma- ent. I'll never be a father!"

She could see that this was a great disappointment for im. It was for her, too. She'd have loved carrying his abies beneath her heart, but she was so relieved that there as nothing serious wrong with him and he really did love ids after all that she couldn't be as sympathetic as she hould be.

"I'm sorry about that," she said, "but what does it have) do with our getting married?"

"What do I have to say to make you understand?" His ne was harsh with frustration as he looked back at the ıfant. "You want children, and I can't give them to you."

"Of course you can," she corrected him gently. "You on't have to make babies in order to be a father. If it's ot too late to prevent her from being placed with another ouple we'll start our family with Dolly. After all, her birth ıother gave her to you. We have a written transcript of the onversation. We'll adopt her and as many more as we feel e can afford to feed and educate."

He frowned and looked back at Dolly. She could see that e still wasn't convinced. "But they wouldn't be *your* chil- ren."

She couldn't hold back a smile. "Yes, they will," she ssured him as she put out her hand and ran her finger ightly down his clenched jaw. "They'll be yours and mine. don't need biological sons and daughters, I just need ba- ies to love and nurture. It doesn't matter who their birth arents are, they'll be ours as surely as if they'd been born) us."

He still looked doubtful. "Are you sure?"

A chill of unease blew across the back of her neck. Was he misunderstanding something here? Was he the one who lidn't want to raise babies that he hadn't conceived? Is that

why he found it so hard to believe that actually giving bir
wasn't that important to her?

Her smile disappeared and she removed her finger fro
his face. "I'm very sure, Rick, but maybe you don't sha
my enthusiasm for adoption. Is that what you're trying
tell me?"

"No!" His tone was adamant. "Adoption would be th
perfect solution, but I thought…" His voice trailed off.

She scooted closer to him so her chest touched his be
knee. "What did you think, sweetheart?" She sound
breathless.

He put his arms around her and drew her between h
thighs. "I thought you wouldn't want a husband wh
couldn't get you pregnant," he said into her hair. "Aft
all, that's a man's main function in the natural cycle
life."

She wasn't sure she comprehended his logic, but she su
recognized the quickening of her body and the hardenin
of his. That was basic enough for her.

She rubbed her cheek against his. "I can't argue wi
the fact that it takes a man and a woman to make a bab
but that's rather low on the list of traits I want in a hu
band."

He sighed wearily and kissed her on the temple. "I don
get you, Jodi," he muttered.

"But you do get me, darling," she insisted. "That is,
you want me—"

"Want you!" He hugged her so hard that she coul
hardly breathe. "I want you so bad I can't bear the thoug
of living without you, but you want children—"

"Dammit, Rick," she exclaimed and pushed herself bac
with her palms on his chest. "Will you stop saying tha
You're the one who's not making sense. I don't want
stud for a husband. I want a man who is warm, carin
kind, generous and loves children. *Loves* children, Rick, n

begets them. Are you going to tell me that you don't love kids?"

He shook his head and cradled her against him again. "I love them. I always have. That's why I shy away from them. Other people's children are too painful a reminder that I'll never be similarly blessed. It nearly blew my mind when the doctor told me I'd never have any."

"I'm sure it was a shock, but why did you lie to me about it? Why didn't you just tell me the truth in the beginning?

"I've never told anyone," he said quietly, "not even my parents."

That jolted her, and she raised her head to look at him. "But why?"

He shrugged. "It's a guy thing, I guess. No man likes to admit that he can't get his woman pregnant. It reduces him as a man in his own mind, and also in the eyes of other men."

Jodi shuddered with distaste. He was degrading the act of conceiving babies to the level of rutting animals.

"That...that's nonsense," she sputtered. "Tell me, if I were unable to bear children, would you think me less of a woman?"

He glared at her. "Of course not, but this is different."

"How?" she demanded.

"Well, it's...it's..." His voice trailed off and he was silent, thoughtful, for a long time.

Just when she'd about decided he wasn't going to answer, he did. "Damned if I know," he admitted. "I guess the whole idea is pretty stupid, isn't it?"

She grinned. "Yes, it is. So, are you going to propose to me, or am I going to have to take the initiative?"

"You can take anything you want from me, my darling," he said huskily, "as long as you agree to marry me as quickly as possible."

With a relieved exuberance she put her arms around his neck and tumbled them both onto the floor, her lips only a heartbeat from his.

"Sweetheart, I thought you'd never ask," she murmured happily just before his mouth captured hers and banished any lingering doubts she may have had about his love for her.

* * * * *